PLEASE WRITE

A NOVEL IN LETTERS

J. Wynn Rousuck

BANCROFT PRESS

ISBN: 978-1-61088-603-1 (hardcover)
ISBN: 978-1-61088-604-8 (paperback)
ISBN: 978-1-61088-605-5 (ebook)
ISBN: 978-1-61088-606-2 (audiobook)

Cover art and dustjacket by Christine Van Bree

Interior Layout by Zoe Norvell

Chapter illustrations by Mary Grace Corpus

Author photo by Jerry Jackson

Published by Bancroft Press ("Books that Enlighten")
4527 Glenwood Ave
La Crescenta, CA 91214
Phone: 818-275-3061 | Fax: 410-764-1967
Email: bruceb@bancroftpress.com
www.bancroftpress.com

To my parents
and all the dogs they brought into my life.

CHAPTER 1

Dear Grandma Vivienne,

You know I only write if something is amiss.

With considerable dismay, I must inform you there is another dog in the house. Frank brought home a puppy. Why??? This is a perfectly contented one-dog household.

The puppy arrived here dirty and shivering in the small hours. Pamela and I were asleep when Frank came into the bedroom, turned on the light, and deposited the muddy pup on the bed.

Pamela sat up, none too happy, and told Frank to get the puppy off the bed and out of the bedroom. And what was he doing staying out until this hour? And where was he? And we cannot keep that puppy! And some other things I didn't catch because I followed Frank and the puppy out of the room.

Frank gave the pup a bath in the basement washtub. It wouldn't stop whining and whimpering. At one point, it jumped out of the tub and shook dirty bathwater all over me. The indignity!

Pamela and Frank need to locate its owners. Soon.

I have enough to deal with trying to keep things on a steady keel around here. We do not need a superfluous, auxiliary animal. It's not even a Boston Terrier.

Yours,

Winslow

P.S. The selfish, scruffy pup has already eaten my dinner, stolen two dog biscuits, and decimated my favorite tennis ball.

DID YOU LOSE THIS DOG?

WHITE FEMALE TERRIER PUPPY
FOUND SATURDAY, OCTOBER 28
IN FRONT OF HAMPDEN 7-ELEVEN

CALL PAMELA: 410-627-0608

Cleveland Heights, Ohio
Thursday, November 1, 1990

Dear Zippy,

My first letter to you! Winslow and I have corresponded for some time, and he wrote to me about your arrival.

What a tough time you have had – cowering wet and cold under a parked pretzel truck in a rainstorm! And what a relief to be bundled into a warm car and taken to a warm home!

I am so glad to have the picture of you that Pamela sent – even if it is on a flyer that says: "DID YOU LOSE THIS DOG?"

I realize the flyer probably upset you. Rest assured, you have nothing to worry about. I promise.

Although Pamela printed lots of these flyers, I would bet that the rest of them are at the bottom of a trash can. Pamela gave them to Frank to post around the neighborhood. But remember, it was Frank who found you and brought you home. He has your best interests at heart.

It is also a positive sign that Pamela has given you a name – especially after insisting she did not want a second dog. I know that she considered naming you "Pretzels." But that might have reminded you of your recent hard times. From what I hear about the way you dash around the house, "Zippy" suits you better.

I also urge you to calm down on another matter. Although Pamela called the Maryland SPCA and placed ads in The Baltimore Sun, she has not had any results. Whoever left you out in the cold – just blocks from the SPCA! – is not coming back. Forget all about him, or her, or them. You now have a brand new, safe, permanent, loving home.

So, no need for worries.

Let's get back to the photo. You are quite an adorable little ragamuffin! You appear to have all of the best characteristics of a West Highland Terrier (positively precious!) and a Jack Russell Terrier (very intelligent!).

I know that Pamela will come to appreciate these fine qualities. Before long.

Winslow informs me that you have a fondness for tennis balls, so I have enclosed a package of miniature tennis balls. They are just your size and may surprise you with some "squeaks." I've also enclosed a rope pull-toy for Winslow because I know he is reading this to you. Be nice to Winslow. Keep in mind that he is a very formal dog (after all, as a Boston Terrier, he always wears a tuxedo). He is also a wise, steadying influence, but he is not accustomed to the high jinx of a young pup. And he was there first.

I am certain Winslow will also come to like you. Before long.

I already like you. A lot.

Love,
Grandma Vivienne

P.S. A bit of advice: Forgive me for bringing up the flyer again. I could not help noticing, however, that in the photo, you are sitting on the leather wing chair in the living room. This is not a good idea. It is apt to make Pamela cross. Winslow never jumps on the furniture.

"Vivienne!

Vivienne!

Vivienne!

Vivienne!

Rope toy!

Rope toy!

Rope toy!"

(Transcribed by Winslow, who requests a new rope toy. Zippy destroyed the miniature tennis balls, then stole my rope toy and promptly wrecked it, too. This is not the way "Winslow will also come to like you" is supposed to work. Far be it from me to cast aspersions, but I am beginning to understand why this pup may have been abandoned...)

Cleveland Heights, Ohio
Wednesday, November 7, 1990

Dear Zippy,

I am told that you have a real knack for getting the most out of toys. It is always fun to have a dog that enjoys toys!

Even so, you should respect Winslow's belongings. I realize that the concept of personal property may be difficult to understand at your tender age, but you must leave his things alone. You need Winslow to be your friend. He knows the ropes - oops, unfortunate word choice – and he is reading you my letters.

Speaking of age, Pamela said you had your first visit to the veterinarian and that he figures you are about seven months old. That is a very nice age to be. In people years, it makes you a toddler.

A word or two about the vet designating you as a "terrier mix." This is something you can be proud of. Owning a mixed-breed dog is new to Pamela, however. Her dad was a dog judge. That means he judged purebred dogs in competitions called "dog shows."

Judging dogs was his lifelong hobby. He began this hobby as a young man, before he got married, and well before Pamela was born. Pamela started going to dog shows when she was just a little girl.

What Pamela may not know is that her father

once owned a mixed-breed dog. He often said it was the smartest dog he ever had.

Pamela's mother also may be partly to blame. After attending dog shows for a while, she began painting portraits of show dogs, which may have influenced Pamela. Her mother put her art aside when Pamela's dad got sick, but Pamela grew up with some of these pictures in the house.

So if Pamela is acting a bit snobby around you, please ignore her. She has been under a lot of stress lately and working way too hard, which is one reason she needs you – to get her out of the office. Did you know that petting a dog can lower a person's blood pressure? That means it improves a person's health. I am sure that just having you around will make Pamela's life calmer. Eventually.

Also, though you may not have loved your visit to the vet, the fact that Pamela took you there is yet another excellent sign that you're here to stay.

To reinforce your place in the household, I have just ordered your first piece of monogrammed jewelry. In a few days, you should receive a package containing a bright pink collar with a tag engraved with your new name, address, and phone number. I know this will look quite chic on you (and I wasn't sure how quickly Pamela would have a tag made).

The tag is shaped like a dog biscuit, but do not eat it! To clear up any confusion, I have enclosed some Milk-Bone puppy treats, with a coupon for Pamela to buy you more.

Love,
Grandma Vivienne

"TREAT!

TREAT!

TREAT!

TREAT!

TREAT!

TREAT!

TREAT!

TREAT!

TREAT!"

(Transcribed by Winslow, who — reluctantly — acknowledges that, yes, Zippy, does appear to be here to stay, as you put it.)

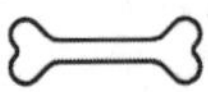

Dear Grandma Vivienne,

Pamela and Frank keep saying how lucky I am to have a

canine companion. I, however, feel compelled to give you a more detailed account of what my life with Zippy is really like. In your first letter to Zippy, you advised her to stay off the furniture.

As you so accurately noted, I (almost) never, ever jump up on furniture. Indeed, I consider furniture-jumping to be behavior unbefitting a Boston Terrier. Zippy recognizes no such boundaries.

She's also the fastest thing on four legs. For several days now, I have had to put up with the ignominy of being chased around the house by this white fluff ball.

Mostly, she chases me around and around and around the first floor — living room, dining room, kitchen, living room, dining room, kitchen, living room, dining room... That would be bad enough, but yesterday she added a new trick.

At some point during this ridiculous race — usually before I have time to notice — she jumps up on a chair or sofa, waits until I come charging by, then leaps on me. The nerve! The humiliation!

Pamela and Frank have reprimanded Zippy about this, but I am pretty sure I detected a chuckle in their voices. Honestly, this is more than a well-bred Boston Terrier should have to put up with.

Yours, the deeply frustrated,

Winslow

Cleveland Heights, Ohio
Wednesday, November 14, 1990

Dear Zippy,

Oh, my goodness. It seems you did not understand my point about personal property. Pamela told me that you chewed up a book, and not just any book – her leatherbound collection of Shakespeare's plays.

I am not going to reproach you. I am sure Pamela has already done so, and I have no intention of adding any "bad dog's" to those you have already received. Fortunately, it is a grandmother's duty to spoil her grandpuppies, not to criticize them.

To be honest, I think all of this fuss about a book is "much ado about nothing," and I commend your choice! No doubt about it, Shakespeare gives you a lot to chew on. Nonetheless, Pamela went on and on and on about her "rare edition." I simply cannot imagine how she expected you to be aware of such things.

Still, Pamela is a theater critic and she uses these books for her job. That job puts treats in the treat jar and kibble in your bowl.

Your job, as I believe I have mentioned before, is to lower the stress in Pamela's life – not to increase it. The lesson here is: In the future, confine your chewing to your toys and stay away from books.

In an effort to channel your chewing in the

right direction, I have enclosed another toy. This toy is in the shape of a rolled-up newspaper: "Doggy News: All the news that's fit to chew." I thought it was appropriate for two reasons: 1) Pamela works at a newspaper, and 2) you are being newspaper-trained.

By the way, you seem to be a smart puppy, so with all of those newspapers on the floor, you might try to pick up a word or two before putting the papers to the use Pamela and Frank intend. This would not only broaden our correspondence, but would take some of the burden off Winslow.

Love,
Grandma Vivienne

P.S. Out of curiosity, which play in the Shakespeare book was the tastiest – "As You Like It"? "The Taming of the Shrew"? "Titus Andronicus"? (Yuck!) Judging from titles alone, I would guess it was "Hamlet."

A note to Winslow: I have put some thought into your predicament concerning Zippy's relay race, and I think I have come up with an idea. After she has made a few circumnavigations, chasing you around the first floor, why don't you just stop? Step aside. If Zippy has built up enough speed, maybe she will just keep going and not notice that you have dropped out of the race. She may even tire herself out!

CHAPTER 2

i heard you
got fixed
didn't know i
was broken
Love,
Grandma Vivienne

Dear Zippy,

All my best wishes for a speedy recovery.

The treats in this package are dog biscuits made by Pamela's mother. They are the best medicine I know. I hope you enjoy them. And do remember to share a few with Winslow.

Feel better soon!

Love,
Grandma Vivienne

Cleveland Heights, Ohio
Wednesday, November 21, 1990

Dear Zippy,

I trust that by the time you get this, you will be back to your peppy self and free of that annoying plastic collar. (Hmmm… Just remembered that these are called "Elizabethan collars." I wonder if your reaction to that pesky collar could be related to your dislike of Shakespeare?)

I know you don't understand what happened to you or why, but I can assure you, it was for the best. Young ladies go through biological cycles that are not much fun – period. Thanks to your visit to the vet, such things need not be your concern. You can focus on what really matters – enjoying yourself and providing non-stop joy to

Pamela, Frank and, I hope, Winslow.

Tomorrow is a Big National Holiday, Thanksgiving – your first holiday in your new home. I am a firm believer in celebrating every holiday that comes along. I have a feeling you will be, too.

Here is a brief account of the first Thanksgiving, in a form I think you will understand:

> Just as Zippy arrived out of the blue earlier this month, pilgrims arrived from across the blue sea a long, long time ago.
>
> The pilgrims celebrated the harvest with the people already living here, the Native Americans. Together, they shared a meal of poultry and corn and pumpkins and all kinds of yummy things.
>
> Every year, we gather around the table to remind ourselves of the good will and fellowship on which this country was founded. (Actually, the good will and fellowship are questionable, but I will save that for a future date.)
>
> Although I have never heard about any dogs at the first Thanksgiving, I am sure they were there, enjoying the bounty.

Pamela and Frank are having guests over

tomorrow. The guests are certain to make a fuss over you, as well they should. I am sorry that I won't be among them, but I will be there in spirit.

I am thankful that you joined Pamela and Frank's household, and I know they are, too. (I told you Pamela would come around!) Who knows? If you give Winslow some peace, maybe he will be thankful for your company, too.

Happy Thanksgiving!

Love,
Grandma Vivienne

A note to Winslow: I spoke with Pamela earlier today and convinced her that, in gratitude for your patience and guidance with Zippy, you deserve the turkey liver all to yourself.

As you are aware, this is our first Thanksgiving without Pamela's father. Holidays are very difficult when you have recently lost someone. I know I can count on you and Zippy to provide some warm, welcome distraction. I will be spending the day with relatives, and I am glad Pamela and Frank are having guests over.

Thanksgiving celebrates peace, and that is what I wish you and Zippy.

"TURKEY LIVER!

TURKEY LIVER!

TURKEY LIVER!

TURKEY LIVER!"

(Transcribed by an angry, turkey liver-deprived Winslow. That fool puppy is even faster than I thought. "Zippy" doesn't begin to describe it.)

Dear Grandma Vivienne,

I wanted to let you know that your suggestion on how to stop Zippy from dive-bombing me worked. Now, however, she's channeling her speed in other areas, such as stealing the turkey liver out of my bowl — just as I was about to enjoy it. The effrontery! The impudence!

And that's only the latest indignity I have suffered. Zippy insists on sleeping in my bed — with me! Not that she doesn't have a bed of her own. But no, she leaps in, shoves me as far to the edge as possible, then sprawls out. When she was wearing that big plastic Elizabethan collar, there was no room for me in the bed at all. I would have crawled into her bed, but I have more pride than that.

Enough complaints about the hooligan hound. Respecting your Thanksgiving wishes, I have vowed to be a peace-maker, and I have made — or rather, am trying to make — peace living with Zippy.

I am writing you now because I need to bring up a more

serious subject, which Pamela may not have mentioned. After the Thanksgiving guests left, Frank also went out. At first, I wasn't too concerned. In my experience, people come and go, often for a few days at a time, without a word of explanation to me. This is particularly true of Frank lately.

This time, though, Pamela seemed unusually upset, which got me worried. She stayed up all night, so I did, too, keeping close watch. I waited by the door for a long time. Then I decided I should keep an eye on Pamela, so I followed her around. Zippy trotted right behind me.

Pamela washed all of the Thanksgiving dishes and pots and pans. Then she scoured the kitchen counters and the kitchen floor. At one point, she turned around and saw the two of us, seated side by side, in the kitchen doorway.

I thought I noticed a little smile before she said, "Are you two keeping tabs on me?"

Then she brought out the vacuum and vacuumed the entire house. This vacuuming spree nearly scared Zippy out of her wits — as if there are wits there to scare. The silly nitwit crawled under the sofa, shaking.

Pamela eventually sat down, and I took my station, lying at her feet. I pretended to sleep, but every now and then I glanced up at her, to make sure she was okay. One of these times, she caught my gaze, leaned down, and patted me on the head.

She sighed and said, "Where is he, Winslow?"

Next she opened the Yellow Pages and started making phone calls. She would give Frank's name, then wait. After a pause, she'd say, "Thank you," hang up, and make another call.

Frank finally walked in the door early the next morning. I was, of course, happy to see him, but he didn't seem happy, and he smelled like the rum cake that Uncle Ed baked for us last New Year's. (I remember that cake because I nibbled some crumbs off the floor. Unpalatable.)

Zippy, noticing nothing out of the ordinary, started leaping for joy. Frank always plays with Zippy as soon as he gets home, but this time he said, "Not now, Zippy."

Ever since then, everyone seems on edge. Except, of course, Zippy, who is oblivious. But sometimes even her comic relief doesn't seem to work. I am sorry to trouble you with all this, but I thought you would want to know.

Yours, a concerned,

Winslow

Cleveland Heights, Ohio
Wednesday, November 28, 1990

Dear Zippy,

I am glad you had a good time at your first Thanksgiving. Pamela said that your jumping abilities are truly spectacular. She and Frank had no idea that you could land on the dining room table in a single leap – from a sitting position! Apparently, their guests were astonished as well.

I am sorry that you were then stuck in the backyard, but I must say, you only made your situation worse by digging up the bulbs Frank planted this fall. It is no wonder that this upset him. That is why, sweet Zippy, after all of your hard work, you ended up spending the rest of the evening in your crate.

That yard is Frank's pride and joy. He built the fancy wood fence himself when Winslow joined the family. The yard has been pictured in Baltimore Magazine. It has been featured on garden tours. It has won prizes. And it is a showpiece for his work as a landscape architect. But you couldn't possibly have known that.

So again, I am not scolding you. That is Pamela and Frank's job. I think you are a highly amusing, creative, smart, and agile puppy.

Here is an idea: I bet you didn't know that Pamela has a friend named Janet who teaches Puppy Kindergarten classes at the SPCA. These would be lots of fun, and they would give you a chance to play with other puppies. I will mention this to Pamela the next time we talk.

In the meantime, I hope you are following my suggestion and paying some attention to the newspapers covering the floor. I think you will be surprised by what you can learn. (And, after the turkey liver incident, I don't know how long you can expect Winslow to continue being your secretary. Boston Terriers may be known as "The American Gentlemen," but even gentlemen have their limits.)

All for now.

Love,
Grandma Vivienne

A note to Winslow: Thank you for taking me into your confidence about Thanksgiving night. You were right. Pamela has not mentioned this on the phone, and it is, indeed, troubling.

In response to your bedtime issue, I am going to suggest to Pamela that until Zippy is completely house-broken, she be crated at night. Not only is crate training an excellent house-breaking method, but it will solve the problem with your sleeping quarters, at least temporarily.

DDDE#$R GHR%A NDFa VIV*IIINEEE,,,,,,,,,I* L)
OPVE# Y&)OU&*&,,,,,, ZZZI*****P_P_Y&

Dear Grandma Vivienne,

You will be pleased to know that I have been encouraging Zippy to follow your advice regarding the written word. But because she barely seems to notice what's printed on the newspapers, I have taken matters into my own hands —

make that, paws — and begun reading to her.

Teaching her to write is more challenging. The enclosed scrap of paper is proof — albeit rather pathetic proof — of my first effort.

This is the method I am using: When Pamela is at the newspaper office, I try to get the pup to sit in front of the electric typewriter. Then I show her that the letters on the keyboard are the same as the letters in the newspaper. You will remember that this worked for me.

The jumble of letters and symbols on the enclosure is the result of my repeated efforts to guide Zippy's paw on the keyboard. This was no easy task. For one thing, she got so excited putting her paws on the keys, she kept hitting them over and over and over again — that is, hitting any letters or symbols that happened to be near the ones I was trying to get her to hit.

Then when the bell would ring at the end of the carriage, she just about went out of her mind with puppy euphoria. She leapt straight up out of the chair and started running around the room until she was too exhausted to continue.

Still, I persevered. But every time she seemed rested up enough to continue, this pattern would repeat. Her few words — and I use the word "words" loosely — took more than forever to complete. All the while, I was afraid Pamela would come home and see me on the desk chair with Zippy at the typewriter.

By the way, her first epistolary effort consists of a mere scrap because she grabbed the paper out of the typewriter with her teeth. This is all that I managed to rip away from her.

Anyway, I have given the matter much thought, and I have a new idea. I'm going to try to get Zippy to sit still long enough to copy a headline from the newspaper. Maybe this will be an easier way for her to make the connection between the newspaper and the keyboard.

You will also be pleased to know that things have settled down around here, although there was a rather strained period during which all of Pamela and Frank's conversation was directed to me and Zippy.

> "Winslow, where did Frank put my overdue library book?"
>
> "Zippy, I hope Pamela knows I can't accompany her to the theater tonight."
>
> "Winslow, do you think Frank remembers that he has a doctor's appointment tomorrow?"

Zippy loved this. Any sentence beginning with her name is cause for unbridled elation, or — if her name is mentioned more than once — chasing her tail.

Now, thankfully, Pamela and Frank are back to speaking directly to each other — and to us, only under appropriate circumstances, i.e.,

> "Winslow, you are such a good dog."
>
> "Zippy, get down off the sofa!"

With order restored, I can devote more time to educating that all-too-easily distracted pup. An uphill battle, to say the least.

Yours, the pedagogically exasperated,

Winslow

Cleveland Heights, Ohio
Monday, December 3, 1990

Dear Zippy,

I am SO impressed by your first writing attempt! I realize there are a lot of distractions – the clicking noise of the keys and the sound of the bell. It is all very stimulating for a small, sensitive canine.

The only answer is practice, practice, practice. And possibly Puppy Kindergarten. Janet doesn't teach typing, but she may be able to help with your attention span.

In the meantime, my repeated thanks to Winslow. I think the idea of copying newspaper headlines is a good one, and I look forward to seeing the results.

Love,
Grandma Vivienne

BNASALTTTIM&&MMOREW SASSSASSSSSSSSUNNM

L:K*(IGGHH%T F(OORR$ AAS:::L::LLL

FAREWWELL TO TRIPPLLLE CROWN WINNNERRR

NORTHEERNN DDANCERRR ONNNE O)F GREAT-TESSS%T HORSSES IIIIN THORRROUGHBBBRRED HISSTORRY

PUUT DDOWWN AT AGE @(

HHORSSE PPUUUT DDOWWN

HORSEE PUUT DOOWN

HHHhorSe HORSSSE DOWNNNNNN

NO NO NON ON NONONONNOOOOOOOOOOOOOOOOOO OOOOOOOOOOOOOOOOOOOOOOOOOOOOOOOOOOOOO OOOOOOOOOO

Dear Grandma Vivienne,

Oh, my. That was a close call. No sooner did I yank Zippy's latest writing sample out of the typewriter carriage than it landed on the floor and that foolish puppy was about to squat down on it. Not that I think it deserved better...

But I digress. I do hope I will not have to provide an exegesis of all of Zippy's writing. This one, however, does require some explanation.

After repeated efforts to make the first two lines legible, I somehow got Zippy to put her paw on top of mine as

I attempted to copy the headline. Unfortunately, sometimes she got excited and pressed too hard or simply wouldn't let up at all.

That, however, was not the biggest problem. Her reading has progressed slightly faster than her typing, but until now, she has not connected the meaning of what she reads with the meaning of what she copies — or at least tries to copy. Today she made the connection.

I take some responsibility for what happened next. I did not use enough care in selecting the headline. Because she seemed to catch on, I took the time to explain who Northern Dancer was and the fate of the poor, old horse.

At that point, Zippy went completely nuts. She started yelping, "No! No! No! No! No!" I thought she wanted to type "no," so I showed her the keys. You can see what happened there. Still yelping, she repeatedly hit the letter "O" until I gently shoved her away from the keyboard. She then started chasing her tail hysterically, which she is still doing.

Well, I guess all of this is at least a sign of progress.

I will continue trying to educate the pup, and I do hope Pamela will heed your advice and send the miscreant to reform — oops, I mean obedience — school.

Yours,

Winslow

Cleveland Heights, Ohio
Friday, December 7, 1990

Dear Zippy,

I am sorry that the newspaper headline you were copying upset you so, but perhaps it is best not to mention that again. The point is, you show real promise — especially for a pup of your youth and inexperience. Keep up the good work!

I understand I may not hear from you for a while because the typewriter is in the repair shop. Pamela mentioned something over the phone about Milk-Bone crumbs jamming the keys. I cannot imagine how that happened.

For now, perhaps you could concentrate on sharpening your reading skills. I know you love to play with balls, and there are many newspaper articles that Winslow could point out to you about people who chase balls. At this time of year, a lot of attention is paid to a long oval ball that's pointed at each end. Almost every big city has a team. Baltimore doesn't have a team now, though.

Maybe there will be more articles about a game played with round balls that are tossed high into nets. Pamela's father, the Dog Judge, loved this game. I think you would, too.

So, play ball! And read!

Love,
Grandma Vivienne

CHAPTER 3

Dear Zippy,

For your first Hanukkah, I am sending you a plush toy in the shape of a child's spinning top. It's called a dreidel. When you squeeze the toy, it plays a song that I used to sing with Pamela when she was small. The song is called "I Have a Little Dreidel." Happy Hanukkah!

Love,
Grandma Vivienne

DdeAr GRRrandMa Vivienne,

Typpewriiiiiiiter iS back! LLeaarrrrrniNg BBBBBBBBBBiig AND litttle letteRs.

Balttimorrrrre SUNNnnn

light FOR aaaaaaaLLLLL

GorBAChev calllllls on TROooops TO police FOOOOOODD supplies

Two FouNd guilty IN FedderaLl PRobe

DReidel IS GUiltY!

baaadd drEIdel! BBBBbaDddddd Drieddel!! ! BbAAd Dreidel!!!!!!!!!!!

DreIdel pOliiice prOBe!

Astrrro LAUnch set FOR tOmoRrow

Crisis iN gulf aggraVates financial SqueeZe

BbbbbbbbbbbbbaAAAAAAAAAddDdDd dreiddddddddel

LoVee,

ZZZZZZZZipppyyY

Dear Grandma Vivienne,

Here we go again. First, allow me to thank you for the

scrumptious Hanukkah dog biscuits. Thank you also for sending them in a separate package so I had a chance to spirit the box away before You-Know-Who could gobble up the contents. This courteous American Gentleman is most grateful.

As you can see, the pup is making some progress in terms of both typing and comprehension. It is a slow and taxing process, but patience is part of gentlemanliness, so I do my best to guide her through the newspaper headlines and explain the broader concepts.

For my part, I thought the plush dreidel was a charming and clever Hanukkah gift. Zippy had a grand time tossing it in the air and catching it, then grabbing it by the stem and shaking it as if it were a rodent. She also enjoyed pushing it under my nose to coerce me to join in the fun, only to grab it away if I made the slightest attempt to pick it up.

But when she sank her teeth into the dreidel and the music started to play, she dropped it like a hot rock, ran under a chair, and whimpered. I have to confess, this was my favorite part of the game; it also made Pamela and Frank laugh, which hasn't happened around here much.

What transpired next will give you an idea of the travails I face in attempting to teach Zippy anything. When she finally crept out from under the chair, she started nudging the dreidel with her nose. Soon she was pushing it across the floor, tossing it, catching it, shaking it, and, oh yes, biting it. At the first few notes of the dreidel song, she became terrified all over again and ran under the chair, whimpering some more. This pup is such a ninny!

I wish I could tell you that she mastered her fears or at least that she learned to leave the dreidel alone, but no. Every now and then, she rediscovers the dreidel and the whole cycle begins again. She then gets so thoroughly rattled (pun intended) by the music that if I try to distract her with headline reading, she starts applying the headlines to the dreidel. I guess that's evident from her sorry excuse for a thank-you note. I attempted to coax her into expressing her gratitude, but the most tolerant of tutors can only do so much.

Pamela says her mother is coming here for New Year's! Zippy and I are very excited, but then, Zippy gets excited about everything. She even wags her tail when Pamela reprimands her.

I, on the other hand, am genuinely enthusiastic about the impending visit. Thank you again for the Hanukkah treats.

Yours,

Winslow

dEEAr gRRAanDmmaA VivieNNei,

Winttter WALlopps WWWWEst

ChEneyy pRRomisses totttall vvvicccctory

CHRisttttmass iiiin cHilee

BBBBBullets edggE Knickss

SOuurrr saucce YUM

Loovee,

Zziippy

Dear Grandma Vivienne,

As you can see, the fluffball's typing is beginning to improve. Slowly. However, I thought her last comment necessitated a few words from me.

Lately, Zippy has developed a fondness for chewing the electric cords. Honestly, I do not know what goes on between the ears of that animal. Pamela and Frank have both scolded her. They tried coating the cords with Tabasco. Zippy found that quite tasty.

They also tried propping the cords up on the furniture, though I can't imagine why they thought that would deter this furniture-leaping, high-jump champ.

It didn't.

Next, Pamela brought home a bottle of something called Sour Dog-Away Spray. She spritzed it on the electric cords, and I can assure you, it was foul. But not to our princess.

Zippy began by licking the cords — a task she accomplished with gusto. Then she became impatient and resumed chewing. Fortunately, Pamela was in the room when this happened or the pup would now be fried fluff.

Pamela ushered Zippy into her crate, put the bottle of Sour

Dog-Away Spray back in the bag, stormed out of the house, and came back later with something called Super Sour Dog-Away Gel. She applied this gooey stuff to the electric cords and let Zippy out of her crate.

Everything was fine for a while, mainly because Zippy flew out of the crate and immediately began running in circles. This went on for some time, and finally Pamela left the room.

Before long, however, Zippy was licking the Super Sour Gel. She took to this stuff with more fervor than to the spray. When Pamela came back into the room, the crazed pup was once again about to chomp down on a wire. Pamela hauled her back into her crate, where the furry nutcase began whining her heart out.

Pamela ignored this. She picked up the bottle of Super Sour Gel and started reading the label. Then she dialed the phone. This is what I heard her say:

"I'd like to speak to someone in charge."

"Oh, good. Hello. I'm calling about your product — Super Sour Dog-Away Gel. I'm afraid, sir, you're not going to like what I have to say. Far from deterring my puppy from chewing, she seems to love it."

"Uh huh. No, I'm not kidding. She seems to think it's some kind of sauce, like catsup or hot fudge, that makes everything taste good."

"Sure. I appreciate that it deters other dogs, but my dog can't get enough of it. I spread it on the electric cords, and she liked it so much, she nearly electrocuted herself."

"No, no. It didn't get that far. I stopped her just in time."

"Never before? Then I guess I'm the first."

"Well, I'm truly sorry if I ruined your day, but I thought you should know."

"Just one other thing: Is there anything else you'd recommend?"

"No, I see. The strongest deterrent. Well, not in my house."

So, that is what has been going on around here. When Pamela's mother arrives, if she smells anything thoroughly disgusting, this will be what it is. Believe me, the pungent mixture of Tabasco, Sour Spray, and Super Sour Gel would put almost anybody, except Zippy, off their feed.

I know Pamela's mom will have a salutary effect on the little darling. I don't want to sound sour myself, but over the past few days, the efforts that Pamela took to keep Zippy from zapping herself seemed... Well, let's put it this way: Puppy Kindergarten cannot come too soon.

I remain yours,

Winslow, the Well-Behaved

Cleveland Heights, Ohio
Wednesday, December 26, 1990

Dear Zippy,

Before Pamela's mother arrives, I think it is time to explain who I am and how I came into Pamela's life. I realize you may be too young to understand, and I am fully prepared to go over this again – maybe again and again. To make my story as easy for you to follow as possible, I have written it as a fairy tale, but it is all true:

> Once upon a time, there was a little girl named Pamela. Yes, your Pamela, but a lot smaller and a lot younger. You might say she was the puppy version of Pamela.
>
> When Pamela was 10 years old, a Big, Bad Disease showed up and made Pamela sick. She was very, very tired and had a very, very high fever. And – though I am sure you will find this difficult to believe – the Big, Bad Disease stole her appetite and she wouldn't even eat!
>
> Pamela's parents contacted Disease Fighters (most people call them "doctors"). They put Pamela in the hospital, which is a lot like the vet's, but for humans. At the hospital, the Disease Fighters gave Pamela a Magic Potion (which is called "medicine"). After a while, Pamela was strong enough to come home.
>
> But she still needed lots of rest, and she wasn't able to go back to school for a long,

long time. At school, Pamela had been learning French (which is a language spoken by people – and Poodles – who live far away). Pamela's mother worried that Pamela wouldn't be able to catch up with her class.

So, faster than you can say, "un, deux, trois" (that's "one, two, three" in French), Vivienne – that's me! – appeared. After breakfast, Pamela would go back to her room while her mother washed the dishes. A few minutes later, I, Vivienne, would show up to help Pamela with her French lessons, and every afternoon we played games and read books and did craft projects together.

Although some might claim that Pamela's mother and Vivienne look a lot alike, Pamela's mother and Vivienne didn't always agree with each other. This was especially true when Pamela's mother would send her to bed for a nap and Vivienne wanted to keep playing. Vivienne and Pamela's mother still have minor disagreements.

Pamela and Vivienne quickly became best, best, best friends. Vivienne is good at keeping secrets, so Pamela could tell her anything and everything, such as how much she missed playing outside and even going to school.

> Mainly, however, Vivienne and Pamela had fun – except one day, when it looked as if Pamela was going to be sick again. Fortunately, it was a false alarm. But on that day, Pamela made Vivienne promise that she would never leave. And Vivienne never has.
>
> So there you have it – happily ever after!

I am going to put this letter down now because I have to help Pamela's mother pack for her trip. Try to pay attention to Winslow's example and behave yourself when she is there. She is not always as understanding as I am when it comes to misbehavior (no matter how amusing the misbehavior might be).

Love,
Grandma Vivienne

Cleveland Heights, Ohio
Sunday, January 6, 1991

My dear Zippy,

Pamela's mother says you are even more adorable than your pictures – that they do not quite capture the pinkness of your tummy. Or the way your expression shifts back and forth between eagerness and confusion. She also said your ears are so flexible, they almost seem like satellite dishes, rotating to catch signals.

She called you "a speed demon" and "an Olympic high jumper." And she laughed when she described the morning you leapt over her lap and grabbed a bagel out of her hand. This is not the kind of behavior she usually would find funny. You must be very cute, indeed!

I was sorry to hear that the noise of the New Year's Eve fireworks was so upsetting. Maybe stealing a half dozen deviled eggs beforehand was not such a great idea – for you or the rug.

Pamela's mother is still rather distressed about the chew marks on her designer boot. Boots may be primarily a fashion statement in Baltimore, but in Cleveland, where the winters are fierce, boots are a necessity. Her first errand after returning home was a trip to the shoe man.

I love you dearly, Zippy, but for your sake, I hope the boot can be fixed. You <u>must</u> learn from Winslow's example. He is not merely an American Gentleman, he is a model of decorum (that means "proper behavior").

From what I gather of your antics, I feel it necessary to address you now as if you were already a mature animal: Pamela is going through a hectic time at work and an uncertain time at home. She needs you to cheer her up, not upset her. That is one reason I suggested Puppy

Kindergarten. This could be good for both of you: Excellent training for you, and an excellent activity to distract Pamela. You might actually enjoy it!

As a matter of fact, Pamela went to charm school when she was a teenager. Lots of girls did and they learned to be lovely, charming young ladies. So if you go to the SPCA's "Charm School," you will be carrying on a family tradition.

All you really need are a few minor behavioral adjustments. I know that Frank already refers to you as "a paragon of puppy virtue" (which, in case he failed to explain it, means an example of puppy perfection). At this point, though, I suspect he says that more to encourage better behavior than as a statement of fact. More than once, I have heard him say: "Fake it till you make it." I am not sure where he learned that slogan, but it is not a bad idea.

I see I have written a rather long letter and am going to stop soon because I also have an important errand to run. I am going to the photo store to drop off the film Pamela's mother took during her visit to Baltimore. I can't wait to see the photos. I am sure at least one will be suitable for framing. I will mail this letter while I am out.

Keep practicing your reading and writing. I await your next letter! I remain,

Your loving and devoted,
Grandma Vivienne

CHAPTER 4

ddeaaRR graMnDMa Vivienne,,,,,

sNOw Days

FiRST WinTEr storM HiTs baltiMOre

cITy SCHOols CLosE

WhiTe sTuuuf falllling frrroM sKy!!!!!

Rolll inn itttttt

PlaY iin iit

CatccH iT

YEA!!!!!!

Fun fun FuN!!!!!!

Brrrrrrrrrrrrrrrrrrrrrrr

COOOOOOOLDD

wettttt

mmmmud

BBATHHHHHHHHH!@#$

&*wWAteeerrrrRR#$%

#$%&*FleASOaP&*(

nooooBEAutyyy parrlorrr !!!!!!!!

NNNNNNNNNoooooooo fun

LLLOvve,

Zipppyy
        yyy
                    y
                          y

Dear Grandma Vivienne,

I enjoyed Pamela's mother's visit very much. I know how sad she and Pamela have been without the Dog Judge. That's how I always thought of him. No disrespect intended, but I never quite recovered from our first meeting when he stuck his hand in my mouth to examine my teeth and then startled me by examining my other end.

I was glad Zippy and I were able to get some laughs out of Pamela's mother, even if every time she so much as attempted to pet me, Zippy started whining and leaping at us. From my point of view, she was overly (and uncharacteristically) forgiving when it came to Zippy's behavior — or should I say, lapses in behavior.

I truly loved the beautiful hand-knitted sweater she gave me (am I correct in suspecting you did the knitting?). I wish I were still the most stylish Boston Terrier in Baltimore. Unfortunately, I was only able to wear this handsome red sweater once.

As Zippy's latest attempt at a letter indicates, she had to be bathed after her crazed romp in the snow and mud. She does not take well to soap and water, even though Pamela tried to calm her down with soothing words about young ladies and beauty parlors. It took both Pamela and Frank to hold the wet, squirmy pup in the laundry tub.

Pamela found this quite funny. So did I. Frank was less amused, especially after he took Zippy out of the tub and placed her on the laundry table. Before he could wrap her in a towel, she shook so much water on him, he had to get a dry shirt. He did not seem happy about this, which caused Pamela to stop laughing.

Frank closed Zippy in the kitchen, and I accompanied her, in a gallant spirit of canine solidarity. Granted, I approach baths with much more equanimity, being blessed with a Boston's shorter, trimmer coat. But I know that full immersion can be a trial, and I was certainly grateful they didn't decide to dunk me, too. Of course, I had the good sense <u>not</u> to roll around in the snow and mud.

But I digress. Back in the kitchen after her bath, Zippy proceeded to leap up and remove my new sweater from the hook where it was drying. She then chewed it beyond recognition. I am thoroughly ashamed of this animal.

I realize a replacement sweater is probably too much to ask for, but should one be forthcoming, I promise that if Zippy so much as thinks about unraveling it, I will unravel her first.

Until then, I remain, as Pamela's mother so accurately put it, a model of decorum,

Winslow

Cleveland Heights, Ohio
Friday, January 18, 1991

My dear Zippy,

Thank you for your enthusiastic letter. I am glad you had so much fun in the snow. Pamela also sent me photos, although I must admit, it was difficult to spot the white puppy in the white snow.

On a related note, however, I am afraid I must scold you. Zippy, I put a great deal of love and effort into knitting Winslow's red sweater. It was not intended to be a chew toy.

Much as I hate addressing you sternly, I feel I must move beyond merely recommending Puppy Kindergarten. It is mandatory – Winslow can explain that word to you if you two are still communicating. Pamela's late father often said: "Naughty behavior may be cute in a puppy, but it is not so cute in a full-grown dog."

As to the bath, I can tell it is not your favorite activity. Considering the rain-soaked circumstances in which Frank originally found you, your dislike of water is hardly surprising.

And, speaking of being soaked, no need to worry about drenching Frank. You were just giving him a taste of his own medicine. (Not literal medicine; it's an idiom, and an idiom is merely an expression). I have suspected for a while that Frank needs to work on his funny bone (again, an idiom — not a literal bone).

However you may feel about baths, I am sure you look quite beautiful - bright white, fluffy, and sweet smelling. As I have frequently told Pamela, you have to suffer to be beautiful.

So, my congratulations on enjoying your first snowfall and surviving your latest bath, though you continue to find the latter closer to agony than ecstasy. The next time I hear from you, I look forward to an account of your first day of Puppy Kindergarten.

Love,
Grandma Vivienne

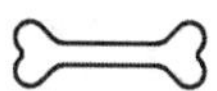

DeaRr gGrrrrramdmmaa Viviennel,,,,

PUPPIEeSS Ppuuppies puPPPPies ppupppieS

run RUuN rrrrrrrunn

chhhhaSE BBBBBBBAlll Chaase bBaalll

RUUUn runnn pupppies rUN BBAll chasse

PUPPIESSSSSS

lLOvee,

ZIppY

Dear Grandma Vivienne,

I am pleased to report that the Dog Judge's wisdom about a pup's naughty behavior hit home. Pamela and Frank enrolled Zippy in Puppy Kindergarten. As you may discern from Zippy's latest epistolary effort, she has already attended her first class.

There was a small glitch at home before class. Pamela was putting Zippy's leash on and kept calling to Frank that it was time for them to leave. Shortly before that, he had been stomping around the house, brushing papers onto the floor and muttering about missing blueprints. Then I saw him head for his truck. I barked, but Frank paid no attention and drove off. (Sometimes getting through to humans can be much more frustrating than getting through to pups.)

When Pamela noticed that the truck was gone, she said

something under her breath, then loaded Zippy into her car and left in a huff. Clearly the right move. <u>Nothing</u> should deter Zippy from obedience class.

Zippy wrote to you soon after she and Pamela got home. Then the pup collapsed into a snoring ball of white fur, where she remains as I write.

As you can see from her recent letters, her writing has improved enough for her to be weaned away from copying headlines. And just in time, because now that she supposedly is house-trained, there are no more newspapers on the floor. I wish I could say there are no more puddles, but that's one more reason I'm in favor of Puppy Kindergarten.

I have enclosed the brochure Pamela brought home from Puppy Kindergarten. You will have to excuse the tooth marks and gnawed edges. There was also a small business card, but it was chewed beyond recognition. Suffice it to say, none of this damage was inflicted by Yours Truly.

Zippy's after-school somnolence is another reason I applaud Puppy Kindergarten. It may be one of the few activities that can actually tire out this canine whirligig.

Well, this bout of letter writing seems to have tired me out, too. There's an unoccupied sunbeam below the kitchen window that looks particularly inviting. I think I'll sign off and take a nap.

I remain yours, the rather vexed but loving,

Winslow

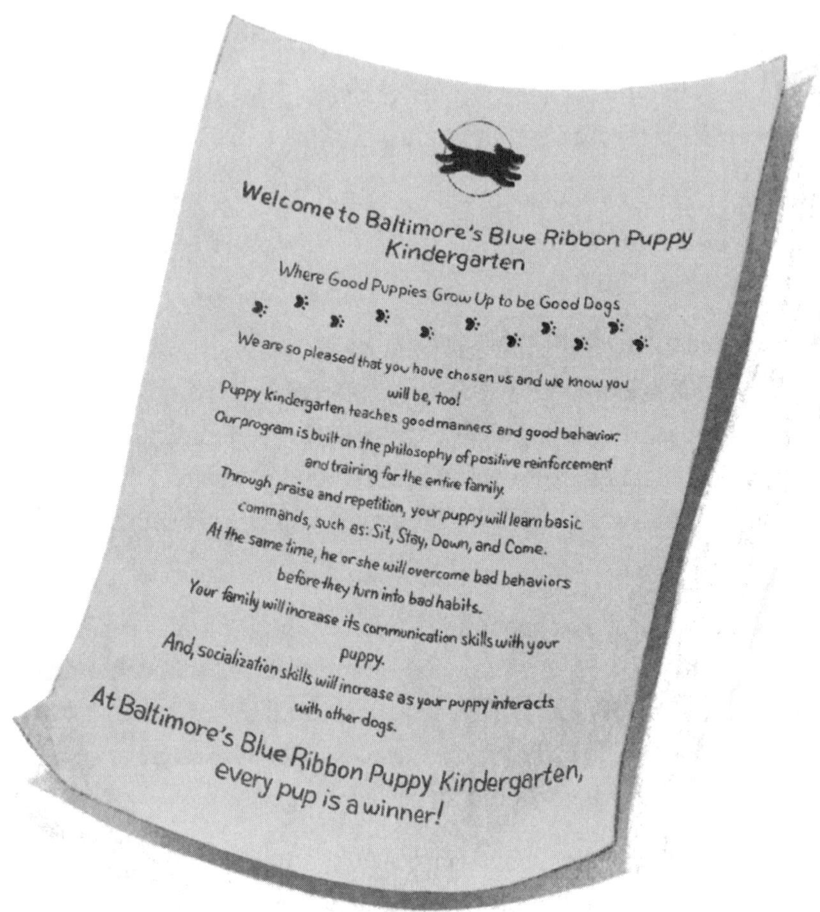
Welcome to Baltimore's Blue Ribbon Puppy Kindergarten

Where Good Puppies Grow Up to be Good Dogs

We are so pleased that you have chosen us and we know you will be, too!

Puppy kindergarten teaches good manners and good behavior.

Our program is built on the philosophy of positive reinforcement and training for the entire family.

Through praise and repetition, your puppy will learn basic commands, such as: Sit, Stay, Down, and Come.

At the same time, he or she will overcome bad behaviors before they turn into bad habits.

Your family will increase its communication skills with your puppy.

And, socialization skills will increase as your puppy interacts with other dogs.

At Baltimore's Blue Ribbon Puppy Kindergarten, every pup is a winner!

Cleveland Heights, Ohio
Sunday, February 3, 1991

My dear Zippy,

In addition to your enthusiastic note, Pamela gave me a detailed account of your first day of Puppy Kindergarten. I am glad you had such a good time!

She said it was delightful to see you running

around with all the other puppies during the get-acquainted period. No wonder you didn't want it to end and refused to come when called. Or stay. Or be caught. Who can blame you for playing a game of catch-me-if-you-can with Pamela long after all the other pups called it quits?

As for pulling on the leash, I realize you are always in a hurry and Pamela seems to be holding you back. I know you like all sorts of important high-speed activities such as chasing squirrels and birds and, of course, the other puppies in class. But maybe, just maybe, you could consider slowing down a bit – occasionally, just occasionally – for Pamela's sake.

Also, please do not fret about the incident in the parking lot. I understand that when a family stopped Pamela and asked if you were up for adoption, she took the father's card and said she would "think about it." But I'm sure she was only kidding. She has been dealing with a great many pressures recently. For instance, I know she was disappointed that Frank had to work and couldn't also accompany you to your first class.

Perhaps instead you should focus on the fuss that the family in the parking lot made over you. With all of those other puppies around, you are the one they called "the cutest dog they ever saw."

I promise to talk to Pamela about this whole matter. I will remind her of your abandonment issues and how important it is for you to have a permanent, stable home.

And so, my darling grandpup, do not worry your fluffy little head about a thing, except perhaps pulling on the leash, and coming when called, and, oh, well, just remember that, as far as your Grandma is concerned, you're perfect in every way.

Love,
Grandma Vivienne

P.S. Pamela says you have been upset by all of the loud noises and bright lights on TV right now. You are going to have to ask Winslow to explain this to you, but the United States (the country in which you live) launched an air attack on Iraq (a country far, far away). Television is reporting on this very thoroughly, and I suspect this is not the end of the loud noises and bright lights. Do not take any of it personally. There is a big difference between bad countries and puppies who occasionally make teensy weensy bad choices.

ddEAr Ggraama fVivienne,,

Lllllast letttEr. Laastt letter

BeInng sHipped away

Shiiped oooofffffffff

too nneww familly

NOoooo nOOo NNNOooO

WWWinslow stAys hoME

ZzippY Ggoes

zzZippy sCaRED

ZZIiipy loovess PAmelaa

HHHHEEEEEEEELLLLLLLPPPPPPPP

ZzziPPy

Dear Grandma Vivienne,

This is not what you, or Zippy, might think. She is not going to live with the family from the SPCA parking lot.

Here is what happened — as best I can piece it together from overheard phone calls, a heated discussion or two, and my own observations. Pamela took Zippy to her second Puppy Kindergarten class. This time Frank came along. Our whirling dervish was so excited, she tried to jump in the car while the door was still closed.

It is my understanding that when they arrived at the SPCA, Zippy managed to get away from Frank and grab another puppy's leash out of its owner's hand. She then started running around at record speed. The puppy at the end of that leash was terrified. (Apparently, it was a Dachshund, and you know how short their legs are. Of course, keeping pace with Zippy, when she's going full throttle, would challenge even a Greyhound.) When Frank finally caught up with Zippy, they were both given a time-out for the remainder of class.

Pamela called her friend Janet, the Kindergarten Major Domo, as soon as they got home. The following is a verbatim transcript of Pamela's end of the conversation:

"Frank and I feel awful about Zippy's behavior in class. We're so sorry. How is the Dachshund doing?"

"Oh, that's a relief."

"Yes, I know Frank should have been at the first class."

"Training for the entire family. I understand."

"I have spoken to him about this, and he promises to attend the rest of the classes. He truly is devoted to Zippy. But we just don't know what to do with her. She seems to be on permanent overdrive. She's just so..."

Long pause.

"...energetic."

"No, you're right. She's very sweet, but she gets so worked up. I'm not sure we can handle her."

"She's so different from Winslow. He was a joy to train — so eager to please."

(I'm not making that up; Pamela really did say it. And, all modesty aside, she's right.)

"Yes, I guess it is the Jack Russell in her."

"You're right. Very different from a Boston Terrier."

"Uh huh, uh huh... But what can we do?"

"Oh, Janet, you would? You'd be willing to do that? For a whole week?"

"I can't thank you enough. In the beginning, I didn't want a second dog, but now I think she can be so good for Frank — for both of us, really."

"Sure, we can bring her to you tomorrow. First thing."

So that's the story. Zippy is spending a week in the country with Janet. My understanding is that Janet is going to evaluate the troublemaker to determine if she is trainable.

Zippy is extremely distressed about this. She kept giving me a look that was partly sad and partly suspicious. (Could she possibly think I had something to do with this — by showing her up, perhaps? Far be it from this gentleman to resort to such underhanded tactics. I merely try to lead by example.)

When it was time for her to leave, Zippy pulled her dog bed under their bed, and Pamela and Frank couldn't lure her out. Frank ended up lying on the floor and dragging out the entire dog bed, with Zippy still in it. Then he deposited Zippy and the bed into the car and they drove off, leaving me with the peace and quiet to write to you.

An entire week of peace and quiet! I didn't want to scare Zippy, but I have a feeling she's coming back chastened, or she's not coming back at all.

I remain yours,

Winslow, The Good Example

P. S. "Perfect in every way"? "Teensy weensy bad choices"? Really?
P.P.S. With all due respect, I would be happy to explain international affairs, or anything else of major import, to Zippy, but getting her to pay attention long enough is beyond the skills of this Boston Terrier. Instead, every time the TV news comes on with its latest report from Iraq, Zippy reacts as if it's brand new. Her latest reaction was to bark non-stop at the television.

dDeear Grandma ViViennn,

EvvaLuaatiiion nno FfUnn!

Workworkworkwork

NiiiiiiCe yeLlow DDog nNamedd teDdy

HHelpPed FinD tYpeeewRiteR

Wedfgbhn

Ghjkpkmesxza789o0

YUJIK

PokjhbgOKJMN

_)(*&

=-[POOHJGBV

OoOOOOOOOOPPPPPPPSs

DROppped TOyyy iiiiiinnnnnN TTTTttttyppppppppewri......

JJJaneT ccCominngg.......................................

Dear Grandma Vivienne,

Enclosed is a letter from Janet, which I retrieved from the waste basket next to Pamela's desk. With due humility, I believe this proves I am not only a fine Boston, but also an excellent Retriever.

In any event, I thought you should see this.

Love,

Winslow

Dear Pamela & Frank,

I wanted to send you a written interim report on Zippy. I think the vet's guess that she is part West Highland Terrier and part Jack Russell may be right on the money. Westies are darling, but they have independent spirits and can have their own agendas... Jack Russells MUST have a job. If they don't have a job, they will make one up.

Combine these characteristics and you get a dog that must be doing something all the time, or will end up doing things you don't want him or her to do.

Training Zippy is going to be a challenge, but at this point, I do think it is possible. It is also important that you do this together. I suspect she knows that Frank lets her get away with things that Pamela won't allow. I will give you a full report, and possibly a demonstration, when you come to pick her up.

We'd love to have you join us for dinner that night, if you're available. That would also give us a chance to discuss some of these things in person.

Sincerely,
Janet

P.S. Somehow Zippy managed to drop a wet rope toy into my father's antique typewriter, and a few strands of rope got caught in the keys. I don't think she did any serious damage, but I'm going to have to take it to the repair shop. I'll let you know what the charges come to.

bBACk hHome BbacK HoMe baCk hOme

YYYYYYYYEAA!!!

PPassEd evalUaTtion!!!

NOw A GOOOD DOGG!!!!!!!

YyeAAAAAAA!

Cleveland Heights, Ohio
Sunday, February 10, 1991

My dear Zippy,

I knew you could do it! You just needed someone to help you channel your energies toward good instead of toward mischief. I was also glad to hear that you behaved yourself during Janet's dinner. That, in itself, was an important test.

And, Pamela tells me that Janet is now using you as her "demo dog" in Puppy Kindergarten classes. She must be an excellent dog trainer!

I had thought puppy training might also be good for Pamela. But with Janet insisting that Frank come along, it is turning out to be a splendid activity for all of you. Pamela says she and Frank are practicing with you every night after dinner. Working together as a family may be the greatest benefit of this training.

For now, my advice to you is: Follow Janet's example in class; follow Winslow's example at home; and I know you will make Pamela and Frank proud!

Love,
Grandma Vivienne

CHAPTER 5

Roses are red,
violets are blue.
Winslow's a good dog.
And Zippy is, too!
Happy Valentine's Day!
Love,
Grandma Vivienne

dDdreAR, Grandma Vivienne,

VaLEntine biscUits

CHHHHHHHHHocolate hhhhhHeart

Uhhhh, oooooohhHHHhhhhhhh

Dear Grandma Vivienne,

Zippy and I thank you for the heart-shaped dog biscuits, which we greatly enjoyed. I'm afraid, however, that they weren't enough for our silly "sweetheart." What follows is: "The Sorry Saga of Zippy and the Whitman's Sampler."

Frank gave Pamela a heart-shaped Sampler. (I think this was technically the day after Valentine's Day. Frank wasn't around Valentine's night.)

Pamela had set the table with a red cloth and candles, and she cooked a fancy dinner — duck à l'orange, followed by coeur à la crème. Then she waited. We all waited. After a while, Pamela stomped upstairs to her desk, pulled out her reporter's notebook, slapped it down on the desk, and started typing. She is working on an article about a play called "Love Letters." This did not seem to cheer her up.

Zippy and I were upstairs with her, of course, but as you may be aware, waiting is not part of Zippy's repertoire. She started bringing Pamela toys — many of them mine, but that's a matter for another time. Pamela kept working and ignored the toys, so Zippy began pawing at her. Instead of shooing Zippy away, Pamela picked her up, held the impatient beast in her lap, and stroked her fur. Zippy actually settled down, and so did Pamela. She took Zippy's face in her hands, looked at her, and said, "Well, I guess it's time for dinner."

Zippy seemed to recognize the word "dinner." She tore down-stairs. Pamela and I followed at a more reasonable pace. Pamela took the duck off the table, cut it into small pieces, and spooned a generous helping into each of our bowls. The duck was tasty, but I didn't care for the orange sauce. Zippy had no such quibbles. She made quick work of her portion, and after I picked out and ate all of the duck in my bowl, she lapped up the remaining sauce, along with some that dribbled onto the floor. Indeed, she licked the floor so assiduously, I'm surprised there's any linoleum left.

Pamela then treated us to large dollops of coeur à la crème, which, if I may offer a suggestion, would be even more delicious spread on a dog biscuit.

Early the next morning, Frank showed up with the Whitman's Sampler. Pamela was not happy with him or his gift. All she said was, "Chocolates won't make up for this." She put the candy on the dining room table, got in her car, and drove off to work.

Frank left a little later. As soon as they were both gone, Zippy made a leap for the candy. When Pamela got home and found the floor littered with empty candy wrappers and the odiferous after-effects of Zippy's binge, I thought Pamela was going to start her own Valentine's Day Massacre.

She scooped Zippy up and hauled her off to the vet, which is where they are now. The pup may have been a comfort last night, but she simply knows no restraint. To paraphrase a song title from another show Pamela has written about, "She's just a dog who can't say 'no.'"

Don't worry about the pooch, though. I'm sure she'll be fine. I seem to recall a similar chocolate incident involving a certain Boston Terrier some years back. He was fine afterward, too, and Pamela forgave him. Pamela's good that way. The Boston I'm referring to learned his lesson. We'll see about Zippy.

Whew. It was a long night, and living through such sagas is exhausting. Time for a well-deserved dog nap.

Yours,

Winslow, The Chocolate Abstainer

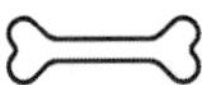

DeAar Grandma Vivienne,

TuMMy AcHe aLL goNe.

BbaCkkkkk In schooool

DEMMo DDOooogg!!!!!!!!!!!

PuPPies do WhaT zipPPy Doesssssss

WWAtcH ZIPpy

FfolLow zZippY

Zzipppy iS GOOOD doG.

LloVVe,,,,,,,,

zIpPY

You are cordially invited to
the graduation ceremonies
of the Winter class of 1991
Blue Ribbon Puppy
Kindergarten

11 a.m., Saturday, February 23

Refreshments will be served

February 21, 1991

My dear Zippy,

I am so proud of you – you will soon be an obedience school graduate! I regret, however, that I cannot make it to your graduation ceremony. It would be an honor to see you receive your diploma, but I am on the cruise ship pictured on the front of this postcard. A close friend of Pamela's mother thought it would be a good idea for her to take this trip (her first since Pamela's father's death). She insisted I accompany her, and for once, I didn't argue. We are currently in the Caribbean, somewhere between the islands of St. Maarten and St. Barts. I will buy you an appropriate graduation gift at our next stop.

Love + congratulations!
Grandma Vivienne

dDear Grandma Vivienne,

nNo DiPloMa!

WHY nOT?

BAD JanEtt!

LOvee,

Zippyyyyyy

Dear Grandma Vivienne,

I guess you're wondering what happened. Suffice it to say, you did not miss seeing Zippy get her diploma after all.

I was in attendance, so I can give you a firsthand account. I will start by setting the scene. Pamela and I were seated outside the ring awaiting the big moment along with the other dogs' family members and guests. The puppies were lined up in a row at the far end of the ring, sitting next to their owners — in Zippy's case, Frank. Janet was in the middle of the ring. As she called each dog's name, the pup and its owner came forward and received a diploma. The diplomas were awarded alphabetically by first name, so You-Know-Who was at the end of the line.

Zippy must have become impatient because, after a while, she began sniffing and turning her head. At one point, she turned it so far, I thought it would go all the way around. I looked over to see what had caught her attention and spotted the refreshment table, just past the ring, not far from where the pups were lined up.

Frank, muttering under his breath, tried to keep Zippy seated in the line and looking straight ahead. Because this caused a minor commotion, Janet kept glancing — glaring would be more accurate — their way.

Then, right after Janet handed a diploma to the owner of a Pomeranian named Xerxes, Zippy broke loose, leapt over the barrier at the edge of the ring, and made a mad dash for the refreshments. Before Frank could catch up with her, she gave the tablecloth a tug, and punch, cookies, dog biscuits, and cups of Poochsicle ice cream went flying. I could tell Frank was about to lose his temper. He grabbed Zippy (in medias res Poochscicle), marched over to Pamela, handed her the pup, and stormed off.

It is a tribute to Janet's skills as a dog trainer that she was able to reduce the ruckus to something short of pandemonium. The result: Zippy did not receive her diploma.

I don't know if a dog has ever failed Puppy Kindergarten before. What's next? Summer school? OED? That would be "Obedience Equivalency Diploma," not "Oxford English Dictionary" — though Zippy could use that, too.

At the moment, Zippy is confined to her crate and whining. Frank took the car and left us stranded. Janet had to drive us home. Not much was said in the car.

Frank must have come home during the night while I was asleep. This morning I heard him tell Pamela he's sure that Janet will give Zippy one more chance, that maybe Zippy can retake the class. Pamela said something about Frank being the expert on "one more chance." I am not sure what she meant, but if Zippy does get to take the class again, you might have another opportunity to attend her graduation.

(I wouldn't hold out much hope, though.)

Your loyal correspondent, the quintessential American Gentleman,

Winslow

Saturday, March 2, 1991

My dear Zippy,

Oh, my goodness!

I believe the correct way of putting it is: You are in the doghouse. Pamela and Frank have invited Janet over to dinner. Maybe they can persuade her to let you repeat Puppy Kindergarten.

It is very important that you be a very good dog when Janet is there. Consider Winslow your demo dog. Whatever he does, you should do.

I hate being so stern, but Puppy Kindergarten is a serious matter. You may be a ball of fluff on the outside, but inside, you are a smart little girl, and I know you can do better.

I also know that you are not really mad at Janet. You love Janet. You just have to remind Janet that she loves you, too.

You can do this, Zippy. I am certain that you can. Follow Winslow's example and all will be well.

We have had a lovely cruise. I will mail this letter from Nassau, our last stop. (The blue paper is airmail stationery.

It is very thin; be careful not to tear it!)

Pamela's mother's friend was right — sailing peacefully on the beautiful Caribbean Sea has helped ease Pamela's mom during the difficult transition to widowhood. A dog can be a great comfort at a time like this, but the family's last dog left us shortly after Pamela's father died. No need for you to think about that, however.

We have visited some fascinating places on the cruise and met some fascinating people — and some fascinating dogs. At one stop, I saw a dog riding a surfboard!

When you are better trained, Pamela and Frank will take you on fun vacations, too. That is something to look forward to.

For now, you must focus on being the best puppy you can be. Put your best paw forward, and I am sure you can work your way back into Janet's good graces and Puppy Kindergarten.

I love you and have faith in you. That's what grandmas are for.

Love,
Grandma Vivienne

P.S. Now that the war in the Persian Gulf has ended, the loud noises and bright lights that disturbed you on TV are over. Surely if conditions in the Middle East can settle down, you can, too.

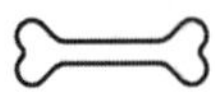

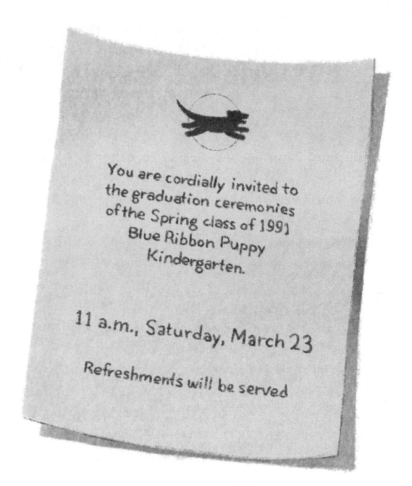

You are cordially invited to
the graduation ceremonies
of the Spring class of 1991
Blue Ribbon Puppy
Kindergarten.

11 a.m., Saturday, March 23

Refreshments will be served

Cleveland Heights, Ohio
Wednesday, March 27, 1991

My dear Zippy,

I knew you could do it! I am so sorry I was

unable to make it to your graduation. (Pamela's mother had an appointment with a doctor – that's a "people vet" – and insisted I go along. No fun!)

The enclosed rubber turtle squeak toy is a graduation gift I bought in the Cayman Islands, where there are many turtles. The other present is for you, Pamela, and Frank together. Think of it as an early gift for your birthday next week. It's a book with a title that already applies to you: "No Bad Dogs."

Granted, you may wonder why you need this book when you have just earned your diploma. Let's just say that it is a handy volume to have on hand. The Dog Judge was a big fan of the author, an English lady named Barbara Woodhouse, who often appeared on television.

I am also enclosing some gourmet dog biscuits that I know you and Winslow will both enjoy. If you get a chance, please send a fuller account of your graduation ceremony. All Pamela told me was that "it went off without incident." Did you receive any special commendation? Did any of the attendees comment on your natural cuteness? I await your report!

Love,
Grandma Vivienne

DeAr Grandma Vivienne,

I miSsed you At gradUation.

FranK And PAmela would Not let me have anY refreshMents.

Why Not?

Man at SPCA Called my diploma a sOciall promotion.

what IS social PromoTion??

What? WHat?? whaT?

I KNOw I No I know I Iknow I knOoo!

ZiPPyy is smARt anD social

smARt and SOcial

socIAl aND smarT

smarT SOCial sMart sOCIal socIAl sMArt smartt SMART

zippy iS a good dOg!

LoVe,

Ziippy

CHAPTER 6

LITTLE ZIPPY'S ONE YEAR OLD,
STILL A PUP AND GOOD AS GOLD!
SHE IS NO ONE'S APRIL FOOL.
OBEDIENCE IS NOW HER RULE.
YES, SHE'S SOCIAL, YES, SHE'S SMART.
LITTLE ZIP, YOU'VE WON MY HEART.
HAPPY 1ST BIRTHDAY TO A GOOD DOG!
LOVE,
Grandma Vivienne

<u>Enclosed note</u>: As you can see, Zippy, I like your explanation of "social promotion"! It inspired me to make you this card. I am sure that is what

the man at the SPCA meant. After all, you worked hard for this diploma – twice as hard and twice as long as the other dogs. And you are nothing if not a social creature.

Also, you should not be concerned that your birthday is celebrated on April Fool's Day. In Shakespeare's plays, the Fool is often the smartest character. Hmmm… Just remembered that Shakespeare is not your favorite authority.

Anyway, I have enclosed some birthday gifts in addition to the Barbara Woodhouse book I sent last week. One gift is something to keep you sweet smelling and the other is something sweet to eat. Pamela's mother made the latter. Enjoy!

Dear GrandmA Vivienne,

Thank yOu for yummY birthDay biscuits.

WanTed tO eaT them All UP.

Pamela maDe mE ShAre WiTH Winslow.

CAKE!!! Zippy also got Cake!

CaKe in mY DishH.

HappY BirThday CAKE!!!

GGoOd dogs sIT.

GooD dOgs Sit quiEtly.

Good Ddogs geT CAKe.

GoOD dogs THinK about chEwing dog book.

gOod dOgs do NoT Chew book.

Zzipppy is A good DOG!!

Winslow SayS i Have tO ThAnK yOU

FoR Doggyy DEOdoRizxzer perffujme.

Don'T like ThaT GIft.

BisCuits ArE beTTer giFT.

LLove,

Zipppy

Dear Grandma Vivienne,

As thank-you notes go, Zippy's effort is only partly polite, and only partly honest. Pamela did tell Zippy she had to share the homemade biscuits. Pamela even put three in my dish. I managed to eat one before You-Know-Who made off with the other two. What exactly did she learn in Puppy Kindergarten? Certainly not the virtues of sharing.

In any event, the biscuit I did eat was delicious — a piquant blend of beef broth and oatmeal with just a hint of — what? Thyme? Rosemary? Perhaps if I had eaten at least one more, I could have deciphered the subtle flavors. Even so, I can honestly say that these treats are much better than the store-bought gourmet ones that Frank occasionally brings home (not that I get to eat many of those) and also better than Zippy's birthday cake (not that I got to eat much of that, either).

As to the dog deodorizer/perfume spray, well, Zippy was excited when she thought it was a scented dog toy. Fortunately, Pamela got it away from her before she punctured the bottle. Frank then sprayed some on Zippy, who took off at warp speed. That animal simply does not like being wet. When it rains, she reluctantly goes down a few of the back steps, then freezes and refuses to go the rest of the way into the yard. She hasn't figured out that if she'd just be expeditious, she wouldn't get nearly so wet as she does freezing there like a statue.

From my perspective, I don't think it's a coincidence that Pamela chose April Fool's Day when the vet asked her to pick a birthday for Zippy based on her estimated age.

But getting back to the subject of dog biscuits, Pamela tells me her mother has published several cookbooks. I wonder if she has ever considered writing a book of recipes for dogs? I, for one, would be happy to be a taste tester. I think you can tell from my above comments that I have a very discerning palate.

Gastronomically yours,

Winslow

Cleveland Heights, Ohio
Wednesday, April 10, 1991

Dear Winslow,

Your idea of creating a cookbook of recipes for dogs is very tempting! I will try to talk Pamela's mother into it. And of course, I would be willing to help. Personally, I would be honored to have you serve as official recipe tester. With that in mind, I am enclosing a sample recipe. It is intended to be an economical alternative to Poochsicles.

See if you can get Pamela to make this recipe for you, then let me know what you think.

Love,
Grandma Vivienne

WINSLOW'S FROZEN YOGURT TREATS

Combine in a small bowl:

- 8 oz. fat-free, plain yogurt
- 4 tablespoons smooth peanut butter
- 4 Milk-Bone Minis, broken into smaller pieces

Mix with a spoon or spatula, then pour mixture into mini-muffin tin or ice cube tray and freeze.

DeaR Grandma Vivienneii,

FrOzen Yogurt tReats

YuMMy yummy!!!!!!!!!

Cookbook should be CallEd

ZIPpy'S CookbOOkk, bY Grandma fVivienne

Recipe iDeas:

CHOcoLatte chippp BiscuItS

TTurkey LIVver SURprise with choCOlate chips

ChOcoLAte Chip SCRambLEd eGGs

LoVe,

ZiPpy

Dear Grandma Vivienne,

Well, guess who ate the lion's share of the Yogurt Treats? Still, I did manage to taste enough to give you my verdict. This is the rare case where I agree with Zippy. They were yummy! I am a Poochsicle fan from way back, though Pamela and Frank haven't brought any home since the debacle at Zippy's first attempted graduation ceremony.

You have found a way to improve on Poochsicles, however, by adding the delectable crunch of the Milk-Bone pieces. This recipe definitely earns a paws-up sign of approval from your recipe tester.

You may be wondering about Zippy's sudden fixation on

chocolate chips. This began when Frank left an open bag of chocolate chip cookies on the kitchen table. Zippy did one of her flying leaps and grabbed the bag, then scarfed down the contents before Frank came back in the room. Delicacy forbids me to go into detail about the physical impact this "snack" had on Her Highness.

She had evidently forgotten her trip to the vet, the one which resulted from her adventures with the Whitman's Sampler. This time, let me just say that the contents did not remain with her long enough to necessitate a repeat visit. And still, she requests chocolate chips. Some animals have a long learning curve.

I feel I should also mention one other thing the fluffball did. This was after she ate the cookies, but before she tossed them. You know how much time and effort Frank puts into the yard. I've heard him say he considers it his "blooming business card."

He recently replanted the plants outside that spend the winter in the basement. The yard looks very colorful and pretty, or rather, it looked very pretty.

Zippy went on a kind of horticultural rampage. I was taking a nap under the tree in the backyard, and when I awoke, Zippy was sitting in the middle of a flowerbed, surrounded by shredded flowers. So, I cannot say for sure whether it was the cookies or the flowers that led to her subsequent gastric distress. I can say, however, that it led to an extremely distressing diatribe from Frank. I only hope the neighbors didn't hear the epithets he hurled at the cowering canine.

Thus, I am afraid there has been some behavioral backsliding on the part of the pup. I have tried to reason with her, but there is only so much a well-meaning, well-mannered Boston Terrier can do.

I probably shouldn't have troubled you with this. Zippy did seem contrite. She hung her head after the effects of the cookies and flowers wore off.

So, no need for concern, but please send more recipes.

Yours,

Winslow, Culinary Muse

Cleveland Heights, Ohio
Wednesday, May 1, 1991

My dear Zippy,

I am almost afraid to mention flowers after my last communication from Winslow. But in the spirit of the season, I am going to forge ahead. Today is May Day, a day that celebrates all of the fragrant flowers, budding trees, and romance of the season. When Pamela was young, she used to make me a May basket, fill it with wildflowers, leave it at the front door, then ring the doorbell and hide behind a tree where she could watch my surprise when I found it.

May Day is also celebrated with maypoles - tall poles with ribbons that hang down from the top. Young people each take a ribbon and dance around the maypole. Because you are so fond of running in circles, I think you would be good at this.

Of course, if you ask Pamela about May Day now, she will probably launch into a discussion of the Labor Movement and workers' rights. That's because she is a member of a labor union - an organization that represents the employees at the newspaper. But political discussions can wait for a later time. If Pamela's union ever goes on strike again, maybe she will take you with her to walk the picket line, an activity I suspect you would enjoy.

For all of the reasons we celebrate the first of May, I hope you had a very happy May Day.

Love,
Grandma Vivienne

DeAr gRanDmA Vivienne,

MOUSE!! MOUSE IN KITCHEN!!! Mouse In DOGfood!!

BBBBBBAAAAAAAAAADDDDDDDDD mouse!

Mouse tRAp! Trap mouse! CCatch mousE!

STIckyyyy as;kjdfgdrthyjkxcvbnope94irjhknlmf

Dear Grandma Vivienne,

Yes, I am afraid we had a mouse in the kitchen. I believe you know my attitude toward these pesky creatures. To wit, I am a dog. I am not a cat. I have my pride. I will not stoop to the level of catching mice. To put it tersely, it is not my job.

I noticed the gray nuisance before Zippy did. It was making repeated forays from under the kitchen sink to the dog bowls and back. This was innocent enough — until Frank put food in the bowls. That's when the furry interloper caught Zippy's attention. The mouse was approaching Zippy's bowl. Zippy charged the mouse, which dashed under a cabinet.

The pup got so caught up in the exuberance of the chase, she practically bounced off the cabinet door, at which point she appeared to forget all about the mouse and launched into another of her delirious races around the house. This went on for some time, during which even the mouse figured it was safe to come out again.

Pamela arrived home at the precise moment the mouse made its reappearance. Pamela was not pleased, not to mention that she almost tripped over Zippy, who was in the midst of her circumnavigations.

Pamela convinced Frank to go out and buy mousetraps. Being a dog of some years and experience, I am familiar with these traps. Pamela and Frank bait them with kibble, but this kibble is not intended for canine consumption. It is embedded in thick glue that can be a real nuisance — don't ask me how I know.

I tried to warn Zippy about this and thought I had succeeded, until I heard an odd "thwacking" noise. After Frank put the mousetrap under the sink, Zippy pried open the cabinet door and got her paw stuck in the glue trap. She then tried to finish typing her letter to you. The last line shows you how well that worked out.

With Pamela holding Zippy to keep her from getting further ensnared, Frank called the emergency vet, who told him to use vegetable oil. Pamela carried Zippy into the bathroom, and Frank followed with the bottle of Wesson's. Every so often, I heard Frank yell, "Hold still!"

Afterward, Zippy was subjected to heavy-duty ablutions. I won't elaborate on the commotion that ensued.

Oh, yes, and what of the mouse? For all I know, it is off notifying its brothers, sisters, aunts, uncles, and cousins that, at certain times of day, there is an unlimited supply of dog food at our address.

Well, all of this has left me in need of a snooze. Catching mice may hold no appeal for me, but catching a few winks definitely does.

I remain,

Winslow — not now, nor ever, a cat

Cleveland Heights, Ohio
Friday, May 10, 1991

My dear Zippy,

I trust you are now fully recovered from the trauma of the mousetrap. (Oh, perhaps I shouldn't have brought up that subject.)

My main purpose in writing this letter is to give you a long-distance pat on the head. I understand that you were of great service to Frank over the weekend when he was sick in bed with a bad cold. Lying down next to him was very smart and caring of you. Not only were you poised to perform any duties he might need – fetching slippers, for example – but you could also serve as a kind of furry hot-water bottle.

I realize that Pamela did not see it this way when she got in bed that night and found you curled up under the covers. (Need I mention that this is something Winslow has never done?) I, on the other hand, think this may be the start of a career for you – Zippy, the Nursing Terrier!

So, even if you were shooed off the bed once or twice – or more – I urge you not to give up. All famous nurses have to start somewhere. And I am sure you are not the first to tend to a patient whose relatives thought they knew more than the medical profession.

Most important, Frank's health is now restored, and I have no doubt that your excellent care had a great deal to do with his speedy recovery.

Keep up the good work!

Love,
Your devoted Grandma Vivienne

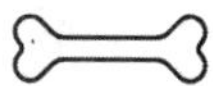

DeaR Grandma Vivienne,

Nursing Terrrier, YAY!!!!!

pAmela calls me A TError.

Nursingg Terrier is bettter!

Send More biscuits.

LOvE,,

ZZIppy

CHAPTER 7

Cleveland Heights, Ohio
Wednesday, May 22, 1991

My dear Zippy,

I am writing to invite you to come to Cleveland Heights for a visit. Pamela, Frank, and Winslow are coming. I know they are planning to leave you in a place called a kennel. They think you might be too rambunctious (that's a big word for "wild," but we both know you are far from a wild animal; you are just a very enthusiastic one).

You need to know, however, that this trip is not exactly a vacation. Pamela's mother has to have an operation on one of her feet. Nothing serious, but it will make it difficult for her to get around for a while, and she wants me to take care of her. I figure I will need all the help I can get, and now that you are embarking on a career as a nursing terrier, I thought this might be a fine opportunity to put your new-found skills to use.

I will discuss this with Pamela and Frank, and I think I can persuade them. In the meantime, think about what you need to bring – your food and water bowls, leash, a few toys. I'll provide the kibble and maybe some new homemade treats.

Hope to see you soon!

Love,
Grandma Vivienne

Dear Grandma Vivienne,

CComing to visit!

Yippeeee!!!

FranK not coming. Winslow not coming. Just ME AND PameLA!!!!

OH, Boy!!!!!

FraNk punished. Stay, Frank!

Is Frank going TO Kennel?

Not ZIpppy.

Zippy is Traveling Nurse.

PAckingg TEnnIs balls and NYlabone and rawhide bone aND KOng anD rope toY AND squeeeak ball and Blue ring AND fAke newsPaper and teniis ballls.

TIme to get in car

Dear Grandma Vivienne,

I am sorry I will not be accompanying Pamela and Zippy to Ohio. I had intended to come, but as Zippy told you, Frank will not be making the trip. He was also planning to come, but something happened.

One night Frank didn't come home again, and Pamela started cleaning and vacuuming and making phone calls. Once again, I stuck by her side. When Frank finally returned (I think it was many hours later; I may have dozed off), he looked disheveled. There was a long conversation about a missing wallet or a stolen wallet. I couldn't quite follow it — in part because when Zippy saw Frank, she started yip-yipping and went into her tail-chasing routine, which distracted me.

The gist seems to be that Frank's driver's license is gone. I heard Pamela say, "What do you expect in a place like that?" Then she told him that if he couldn't drive, she might as well go by herself, and maybe she'd take Zippy along for company and comic relief. While I was surprised by this, I have to admit that Zippy's antics are, if nothing else, silly.

The conversation stopped there — except for Zippy, whose

yipping turned to barking when she heard her name. Pamela issued one stern, "Zippy, settle down!", and went into the den to work. Frank went to bed.

I am so disappointed that I won't be seeing you. I have fond memories of previous trips to Cleveland, when the Dog Judge was alive and used to say things like: "You know, Winslow could have been a champion if he'd had a professional handler." But then, my dog show opportunities are long past. There's no point dwelling on what might have been. I wonder what he would have thought of Zippy.

Mostly, I will miss being there to give you moral support as you help Pamela's mom through her recovery. Zippy does seem to be demonstrating a minor talent for nursing care, so perhaps she actually can be of some service. Do know that I will be thinking of you. For now, it seems I will be taking care of Frank, who appears to be at a low ebb. I hope my conscientious support and presence will help bolster his spirits.

With all best wishes that everything goes smoothly,

Winslow

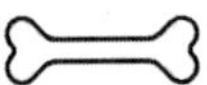

Cleveland Heights, Ohio
Monday, June 17, 1991

My dear Zippy,

Thank you for coming to visit and helping

care for Pamela's mother. I realize you were bored when you were left alone in the house while we were at the hospital. As I understand it, dogs do not have the best sense of time, or even a sense of whether their owners are ever coming back.

With that in mind, I do not think you should be blamed for overcoming your boredom and anxiety by, well, let's call it "antiquing" the dining room chairs. I realize Pamela doesn't want her mother to know about this, so I will leave it at that.

Her mother, however, did appreciate your cheery welcome when she came home. Seeing you leap in the air and perform a free-form doggy dance was good medicine in itself, especially after throwing an embolism caused her to spend a week in the hospital.

And though she was also amused by your talent for bouncing a ball off the wall and catching it, she was less amused, after you were back in Baltimore, to find the spots this diversion left on the wainscotting.

That aside, your presence was a balm ("balm" has nothing to do with "ball"; Winslow can explain). You truly are 15 pounds of fur-covered happiness, as Frank puts it. And I think you could brand what he calls your "on-the-patient care."

That's all for now. When minor surgery turned into a major emergency, it left Pamela's mother needing more help than anticipated. She still gets rather tuckered out.

With gratitude for your nursing services and, as always,

With love,
Grandma Vivienne

Dear Grandma Vivienne,

Why noT ALL BEetter?

Not Zippy"S fault!

WHat is throwIng an EMboliXsm?

Zippy is good AT playing Catch.

Zippy can catch balls. RuBBer balls. TEnnis balls. Squeak balls.

Zippy tried to catch emboliSm.

COuldn't find it.

iSs Zippy A BaD nurseE?

Nooo!! GRandma Vivienne Says Zippy is a Good nUrse.

Tell PAMel'as mother to feel Better!

Now!!!

Zippy did not huRT furniture.

wHEn FRank does not CoMe home, Pamela moves Chairs to vaccUUm.

ZIppy hatES vacuujm, so ONly moved ChAirs.

With teeth.

dId not hurT Chairs.

Lvee,

Zippy

Dear Grandma Vivienne,

First, allow me to say how pleased I was to learn that Pamela's mother is home at last and doing better. What a scare! I do regret that I could not be with you. For one thing, I could have helped out at the house, particularly when the visit had to be extended. As you correctly ascertained, Zippy is not accustomed to being left alone, though that is no excuse for the dining room disast... oh, my, Pamela said, "Let's not dwell on that." The important thing is that Pamela's mother's health is improving.

Frank added a new activity to our daily regimen while Pamela and Zippy were in Cleveland. Every morning before work, he goes to a church basement and sits around talking to a group of people. I know this because after a day or two, he started taking me with him. The church is about two blocks away — a lovely constitiutional, although Frank never lets me fully indulge in all of the tantalizing new smells along the way.

The folks at the church seem very nice. They always set out a bowl of water for me, and just about everyone bends down to pet me on their way out, as they're saying, "Keep coming back." I hope we do. Frank seems quite earnest about this activity, and we both appreciated the company when we were on our own.

In his spare time, Frank has also started doing a landscaping project for a treatment center somewhere out in the county. He works on blueprints on the dining room table after dinner. Then on weekends, he loads up his pickup with bags of mulch and small bushes and trees and flowering plants. He has sworn me to secrecy on all of this. I think he's waiting to show Pamela the finished gardens. I'm sure she'll be proud. She always says he's the most talented landscape architect in town.

Frank and I missed Pamela — and maybe even Zippy — while they were in Cleveland. Frank also did a lot of work around the house and yard and put a vase full of flowers in the bedroom for Pamela. We're glad they're both home.

Yours,

Winslow

Cleveland Heights, Ohio
Sunday, June 23, 1991

My dear Zippy,

Pamela's mother is feeling better every day. Sometimes it takes people a while to recover. Please know, little pup, that this is no reflection on your excellent nursing skills.

I am accompanying her to physical therapy, and I am sure that will help her continue to get stronger.

One of your bits of mischief was actually an example of good nursing. Attempting to chew up a carton of cigarettes showed your deep concern for Pamela's mother's health, even if the outcome of your efforts created stains I am still trying to get out of the carpet. Pamela's mother has not noticed the stains – or the teeth marks you left on the dining room chairs – but I am dismayed to tell you that I did catch her searching for the cigarettes.

Smoking is a terrible, dangerous habit. The doctors had no doubt it contributed to the embolism. But as I do not have to tell you, dear pup – and I mean this in the most loving way – bad habits can be difficult to break.

On a more cheerful note, I understand that you thoroughly enjoyed your car rides to and from Cleveland. I was very impressed by the seatbelt/carseat contraption that Pamela found for you. She said that, within minutes of hopping in, you had licked the passenger window so completely, it looked frosted.

There is a great book called "Travels with Charley" about a famous author whose driving companion was a dog (a Standard Poodle). The book is probably too advanced for your reading skills right now, but maybe I can read some of it to you the next time we're together.

I hope that won't be too far in the future. I miss you and Pamela very much.

Love,
Grandma Vivienne

P.S. I am sorry that Pamela missed more work than she expected and is scrambling to catch up, but this gives me an idea. Now that you have become such a literate little creature, perhaps you could help with her research…

DeAr Grandma Vivienne,

Zippy is Good nurse After all!

Knew it!

You bet Car ride WaS fUn!!!

SIT nexT tO Pamela.

LOoK oUt windoW.

Put paws on arm rest.

PUt paw on button, window goes down!

Window UP! Window down!

Stop that, Zippy!

Drive past Houses treees TRucks bUs TTRees cARs, dogs, Dogs in Cars!!!

Bark hello At dogs in cars.

ZiPPy setttle Down NOW!

Car ride tiring.

Zippy has job.

Real joB!

Zippy is REsarch ASsisTant.

ANNIe gEt YouR Gun...

YoU Can"'t Get a mAn with a Gun

ANYYThingg yoU Can DOO i Can do BBEtttttttttt

loVEE,

ZIpPY

Dear Grandma Vivienne,

I think the end of Zippy's letter needs a few words of explanation. After she returned home, Zippy took your suggestion about helping Pamela with her work and ran with it — as is her wont. Being Zippy, her brand of "help" can be a tad over-zealous. When Pamela sits on the easy chair in the den and reads, Zippy jumps on her lap, often knocking books and papers to the floor. On at least one occasion, when Pamela tried to retrieve a book, Zippy grabbed it and tore around the house with the book in her mouth.

She has also become fascinated by the stereo. Pamela was working on a review of "Annie Get Your Gun," and when she put the record on the stereo, Zippy went running from one speaker to the other. I was beginning to think she might be related to RCA's Little Nipper. Then she batted a paw at the turntable and knocked the arm across the record. (Little Nipper would never have done that.) Prior to the stereo incident, however, Frank observed Zippy "assisting" Pamela and dubbed her Pamela's "research assistant."

He also brought Zippy and me along with him when he showed Pamela the landscaping work he did at the treatment center. Zippy was so excited to be in the car, I don't think she fully appreciated his artistry with the grounds, but I did, and Pamela did, too. She had tears in her eyes when she saw what Frank had been up to while she and Zippy were in Cleveland. Then Zippy starting digging in one of the flower beds and Pamela quickly deposited her back in the car, where the scruffy pup proceeded to get mud all over the backseat. Pamela and Frank didn't seem to notice.

This observant correspondent thinks it isn't just Pamela's mother who's getting better. Frank and Pamela also appear to be on more solid "ground" (pardon the landscaping pun). And speaking of "better," anything Zippy can do, I can definitely do better!

Yours,

Winslow

Cleveland Heights, Ohio
Tuesday, July 2, 1991

My dear Zippy,

What wonderful news – you are going to have an addition to your family! I will try to explain this news in terms you can understand.

Pamela and Frank are expecting a baby. A baby is a kind of people puppy, although a baby takes much longer to grow up than a puppy does. The period between being a people puppy and being a grown-up is called childhood, and this will be a really fun time for you.

Pamela's late father felt strongly that all children should have dogs. More than once, he presented a dog to a child in a dog-less home. Admittedly, this sometimes produced mixed results, especially because he liked the puppy to be a surprise. Years ago, he surprised his nephews with a Cocker Spaniel puppy. They were overjoyed, but their mother was not. I won't go into all of that here. Let's just say that was how Pamela came to own a Cocker Spaniel, and a lovely dog she was.

But back to how Pamela and Frank's news will affect you. For a while, you will not be allowed to get too close to the baby. But when the baby gets a little older, you will have a splendid playmate – a friend for life. In other words, you are a lucky dog, indeed. So, congratulations to you, too, Zippy!

I don't know whether I should mention this, but on Saturday night Pamela's mother seemed to be having a relapse – that's when an illness returns unexpectedly – and she had to go back to the hospital. It turned out to be a false alarm and she was home the next morning. Then Pamela called, and her baby news lifted her mother's spirits better than any medicine. It's great news for everyone.

Love,
Grandma Vivienne

DeaR Grandma VivvienE,

People pupppy!!!

PLAymate for life!

WHeree is peeople puppy?????

Have loooked everywheRE.

UndEr bed

in closets

uNder sofa

STUCk under sofa stuck uunder sofastuCK under sofaaaaa stuuck under soooffa stuckstuckstuckstuckstuckstuck-stuckstuckstuckstuckstuckstuck

HEELLPP!! PAMELA!!!!

WeHre IS people puppY?????

lOVe,

zIPPPy

Cleveland Heights, Ohio
Wednesday, July 10, 1991

My dear Zippy,

I see that the explanation in my previous letter did not go far enough. The people puppy will not be here for many months, after the leaves have turned color and fallen off of the trees, after the snowflakes have fallen and started to melt. That's when the baby will arrive.

Even actual puppies take a couple of months to appear. People puppies take longer than that. I am sorry if I caused you frustration by building up your expectations too soon.

I know there are already so many frustrations in your life – not being able to reach the food Pamela puts on the counter, not being able to ride in the car every time Pamela and Frank go for a drive, not being allowed to eat the kibble in Winslow's bowl. I apologize for adding to this list.

Pamela told me about the sofa incident. She said you normally dash around the house so enthusiastically, she didn't think anything of this particular mad dash. As Pamela's research assistant-in-training, you should know that when you see Pamela sit down with a pile of books, she is working and should not be disturbed.

In this case – and of course there's no way you could have known this – Pamela had gotten a very important, very last-minute assignment to interview a very famous playwright. His name is Edward Albee and he owns Irish Wolfhounds. (Pamela always finds out what kind of dog her interview subject has; that's called in-depth research and it's one of the things I thought you could help her with.)

She was just about to leave to meet Mr. Albee when you got trapped behind the wood rails at the base of the Chippendale sofa. You are lucky she heard your frantic scurrying. Otherwise, you could have been stuck there for hours.

You do have to be more careful, Zippy. Pamela is not supposed to be moving furniture these days. Especially now, it is important that you try to provide the type of quiet companionship that Winslow does. Have you noticed the way he lies at Pamela's feet when she is working? That would be an excellent example for you to follow.

I hope this letter helps you understand more of what's going on, what to expect, and when. Perhaps I should not have told you about the people puppy so early. I just couldn't resist sharing my own excitement.

Speaking of excitement, Pamela said the July 4th fireworks made you more excited than frightened. She said you were leaping so high in the backyard, she thought you were going to catch one of the fireworks. Come to think of it, you are something of a firecracker yourself. So, belated happy Independence Day!

Love,
Grandma Vivienne

CHAPTER 8

Dear GRandma Vivienne,

Winslow and ZZippy going to CAMp.

WHat IS camP???

DDon'T want to Go!

WON'T GO

wILL NEVer come HomE.

HHapppy at home.

Won't leave home.

NO CamP NOCamPNocampnoCamp noCAmP NoNONOOoo campppp nononononNOooo

Lovvve,

ZZIPPYYY

Cleveland Heights, Ohio
Wednesday, July 17, 1991

My dear Zippy,

I hope you have settled down by the time you receive this letter. I am sending some reassurances – just in case. Camp is a fun place that only very fortunate, very good dogs get to go to. It is a treat. (No, that may confuse you. It is not the kind of treat that you eat.) It is a privilege, a present.

Pamela has told me all about this camp. She researched it, and then she visited it. It is located in the country with lots of trees and grass and sunshine. It has a puppy pool in which you can splash around with the other dogs – if you have changed your opinion of water, that is. And there will be lots and lots of other dogs to play with. Plus, you will be there with Winslow.

Pamela is also going to pack some of your favorite toys and biscuits and food. So there will be lots of familiar things and many fun new things.

Most important, camp is just a mini-vacation for a limited amount of time. You and Winslow will definitely be coming home after camp.
I understand why this concerns you, but this is not something you should worry about.

You are going on this mini-vacation so that Pamela and Frank can go on a mini-vacation of their own. They are going to a place called Anna Maria Island, off the coast of a state called Florida, and unfair though it may seem, the inn where they are staying does not allow dogs.
I know they will think about you a lot while they are away. Maybe they will call you on the telephone. But they do need – and deserve – this time away by themselves.

While they are having a good time, you will be having a good time yourself. Then they will come and get you. I promise. So, no more complaints, please. Just focus on how much fun you are going to have.

Love,
Grandma Vivienne

Dear GRandma Vivienne,

CAMP Is baD!!!

HATe camp

Bbad camP

POoodle took Zippy'S Ball.

ZIppy TOoK pooodle's boNE.

POODle chased Zippy.

Poodle growwwled

ZIPpy Barked

Zippy got TIME OUT.

NOT Poodle.

WANt to go home.

UH oh. Using office typewriteR.

NO DOgs ALlowed in Office.

Hear cOUnSelor coming.

WANT TO GO HOME!!!!!

time out.

lovve,

Zi

P

p

y

Cleveland Heights, Ohio
Wednesday, July 24, 1991

My dear Zippy,

I see that you are not finding canine camp as much fun as I – and especially Pamela and Frank – hoped you would. Part of the problem may be that, no matter how the Poodle behaved, you continue to lack a clear sense of personal property. Pamela might actually approve of this because she believes in sharing the wealth. But that is a discussion for another day.

I hope this care package will cheer you up. Pamela's mother came up with two new biscuit recipes. The ones shaped like bones are peanut butter and wheat germ. The round ones are oatmeal carob chip. (They look like chocolate chip cookies, but these are actually good for you.) Please ask Winslow to send me his reviews.

You will notice that this is a very large package. It includes big batches of these treats so you can share them with the other dogs – not just Winslow, but all of the dogs, including the Poodle. This should help get you back in the good graces of the Powers-That-Be at camp.

I received a picture postcard of Anna Maria Island from Pamela and Frank. They are having a nice, relaxing trip. Pamela wrote that she called the camp and they put the receiver up to your ear. She said all she could hear was whining.

Zippy, you, too, need to relax. You cannot come home until Pamela and Frank come home, which is just a little more than a week away. So focus on having fun and remember to share this care package.

Love,
Grandma Vivienne

DeaR Grandma Vivienne,

ZIppy only got 2 treats.

COUNseLors GAvE eveRY DoG 2 TReats.

Package ADDressed to ZIPPY

senT To Zippy

NOT FaiR.

HATE CAMP.

WANT to go Home.

cOme geT Zippy.

Winslow says tO say tHanKs.

THAnks.

Winslow Wants tO writE SOMething.

LOVe,

ZIPPy

Dear Grandma Vivienne,

I will try to make this brief because we have sneaked back into the camp office to use the official typewriter, which is strictly off limits. However, I appreciate your asking for my review of the latest recipes and feel duty-bound to respond promptly while the various flavors remain fresh on my palate.

My short response is that the treats were delightful. I am not a fan of carob, but I found the shape and texture of the oatmeal carob chip batch extremely pleasing. I also commend Pamela's mother on the peanut butter-wheat germ treats. If you don't mind passing along a suggestion, though, I wondered if she would consider using chunky peanut butter instead of smooth. It would give the treats added texture and crunch, which I think would make a scrumptious biscuit even more so.

Zippy and I had better hightail it out of here before we both get time-outs. I do think her typing is getting better, don't you? She still needs to work on upper and lower case letters, but she's starting to write some full sentences.

On the other hand, after your treats were distributed, she found the trash can containing the empty box, knocked it over, pulled out all of the contents, and started shredding the box. I try to keep an eye on her, but even the most well-intentioned Boston Terrier can only do so much.

Oops. I think I hear someone. Have to run. Thank you again for the treats.

Yrs,

W

Dear Grandma Vivienne,

YAHOo!!!!!!

Home from CaMp early!!!!!

FRank came and got us.

SO Happy to See him!!!!

SO HAPPY

SO happY

So HAPpy

FrAnk less happy.

Why?

LOve,

Zippy

CHAPTER 9

Cleveland Heights, Ohio
Friday, August 2, 1991

My dear Zippy,

I see how thrilled you were to get released from camp early. I know you probably think this happened because you complained. Surely you have noticed by now, however, that Pamela has not gone back to work, but has been home in bed.

I do not want to frighten you, but you should know that while Pamela and Frank were on vacation, Pamela had a small health scare and that is why they came home early. Pamela's doctor doesn't think this is anything serious, but he wants her to rest in bed for a while.

This is where the skills of Zippy, the Nursing Terrier, can come in handy again. Keep Pamela company and cheer her up. She might even let you up on the bed for a cuddle. In your enthusiasm to help, however, make sure you do not jump on her. Just lie quietly by her side, and I am sure you will prove a great help as well as a cheerful distraction. I am counting on you, Nurse Zippy!

Love,
Grandma Vivienne

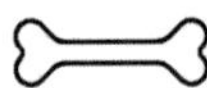

DeaR Grandma Vivienne,

Zippy on time-out aT HOME

UNFAir!!!

TIME-out in the kitchen

This is my story:

Box came to front door

Zippy's job:

Inspect andd Protect

Sniff box

PAW at box

PUsh box

Flowers sticking out of Box.

SuspiciouS.

FRank brings box in

Stop thaT, Zippy!

FRAnk puts Flowers on table.

Zippy Inspects and ProtecTS.

JUMp on Chair

WALk across tablE

SnifF Flowers

TASte floWERS

Eat FLoweRS

TIME-OUT!!!

Pamela and FRank

WATching Law and Order

IN bedroom.

Zippy likes LAW And ORDeR.

UNfaiR punishment.

LovE,

ZIppY

Cleveland Heights, Ohio
Friday, August 16, 1991

My dear Zippy,

What a long letter! I am pleased that you put your time-out to such good use, and that you are learning so much from watching television with Pamela and Frank. Pamela's mother and I enjoy watching "Law & Order," too.

Now to the flowers. Zippy dear, those flowers were a get-well gift from Pamela's mother. I appreciate your vigilance in checking out everything that arrives at the door. However, I believe you overdid it this time. Sniffing is one thing. Destroying is another. I regret to say that I think you deserved this time-out.

On a happier note, I was pleased to learn that Pamela has gotten the okay from her doctor to return to the newspaper on Monday. Clearly your nursing skills had a positive effect.

Now you and Winslow can go back to your regular routine of guarding the house and resting up so you can be in tip-top form when Pamela gets home from work every day.

By the way, please tell Winslow that Pamela's mother followed his suggestion and replaced smooth peanut butter with chunky in the recipe for the peanut butter wheat germ treats – an excellent recommendation. I have enclosed a few samples as well as a copy of the recipe.

All for now.

Love,
Grandma Vivienne

CHUNKY PEANUT BUTTER WHEAT GERM TREATS

- 2 eggs
- ½ cup oil
- ½ cup water
- ⅓ cup chunky peanut butter
- 1 cup oats
- 1 cup wheat germ

Mix wet ingredients together. Stir in dry ingredients. Roll out ball of dough. Cut out bone-shaped biscuits with cookie cutter. Bake at 375 degrees for 20 minutes.

Dear Grandma Vivienne,

Zippy and Pamela anD FRank and Winslow

went to big party in park.

Lots of people.

Lots of food on ground.

Hot dogs And popcorN ANd COtton candy and CokE And peanuts and

Zippy's tumMy hurts.

Uh oh.

Much better Now.

All better now.

OOps. Uh oh.

Got to go.

Love,

Zippy

Cleveland Heights, Ohio
Wednesday, September 4, 1991

My dear Zippy,

How nice that Pamela and Frank took you and Winslow to a Labor Day union rally on Monday! I am glad the four of you enjoyed this family event together. As you may remember from my explanation of May Day, Pamela is a strong believer in the union movement. Pamela's union makes sure that workers get all the rights to which they are entitled – rights like fair pay, which helps put kibble in your bowl.

She told me you marched wearing a Newspaper Guild bandana around your neck and joined in with a few barks during the cheers and applause for the speakers. She said she was proud of you.

Tomorrow would have been Pamela's father's 80th birthday. He often judged dog shows on his birthday because it frequently occurred during the long Labor Day weekend. He was a very fair and well-respected judge, and he certainly knew a good dog when he saw one. I think I have told you that Pamela's mother used to paint portraits of some of these dogs. She has not done one in a long time, but maybe she will paint a portrait of you someday!

You are quite different from the dogs Pamela's father used to judge. Many of them looked a lot like Winslow. But I am sure Pamela's dad would have gotten a kick out of you. I know I do.

Again, I congratulate you on your model behavior during the rally. Here's to people and puppies: Solidarity Forever!

Love,
Grandma Vivienne

Dear Grandma Vivienne,

Dog Judge???

Dog Judge would kick Zippy???

Zippy is not guilty!!!

Zippy is a good dog!!!!!

Zippy WatcheS Law anD Order

zIppy waNts a lawyer.

Will not take a plea.

did not do it.

DO What???

What is the charge??

Zippy will not go to jail!

GrandmA Vivienne must be character witness.

ZIPpy is innocent!!!

Love,

ZIPpy

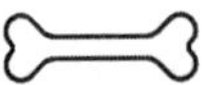

Cleveland Heights, Ohio
Friday, September 13, 1991

My dear Zippy,

Oh, my. It seems that I have a good deal to explain to you, starting with the meaning of "to get a kick" out of something. This has nothing to do with actually getting kicked. It's an expression that means "to enjoy" something. Pamela's father, the dog judge, would have enjoyed you. He would never, ever, ever have kicked you.

That brings me to explaining what a dog judge is. I thought I had mentioned this to you once before, but it was when you were a young pup and easily distracted. So I will try again.

A dog judge is not the type of judge who punishes pups and puts them in jail. Quite the opposite. A dog judge awards prizes to purebred dogs.

The dogs' owners or handlers parade the dogs in front of the judge. He then examines the dogs and decides which one comes closest to the ideal – called the "standard" – for that breed.

Because you are a mixed-breed terrier, you would not be allowed to compete, so you need not trouble your fuzzy little head about such things. Indeed, there is no standard for a Zippy dog. You are, quite simply, the best Zippy you can be. So in that sense, I guess you could say you are always "Best in Show."

Come to think of it, there is an event in which you could compete – an agility trial. (Don't worry. This is not the kind of trial you see on "Law & Order.") It includes lots of fun equipment, such as a seesaw, a tunnel, and poles to weave in and out of. I will ask Pamela and Frank to see if they can sign you up for agility training. I'll bet you will "zip" right through it!

I am glad that watching "Law & Order" together has become a regular family activity. But please be assured that Pamela's father was a different type of judge entirely. He judged dog shows because he loved dogs. And though the dogs he judged were different from you, I am sure he would have come to love you.

Try not to worry so much, Zippy. For Pamela and Frank's sake – as well as your own – try to focus on being a happy pup and bringing happiness to others. You have a real knack for that.

Love,
Grandma Vivienne

dEar Grandma Vivienne,

Zippy started aGility class.

Zippy loves tunneL!!!

Went in tgunnel.

Ran in circles in tunnEl.

Stayed in tunnel.

Tunnel is fun!

Teacher CrawLed in Tunnel

Dragged ZIppy out.

Zippy rAn back In.

Ran iN more circLes.

Won'T come Out.

Fun in Tunnel!!!

TEAcher crawlled back IN.

Took Zippy out.

ZIPPy ran in Again.

Fun fuN Fun game!!!

Teacher Back in tunnel.

Zippy no longer in Agility class.

lovE,

Zippy

Cleveland Heights, Ohio
Friday, September 27, 1991

My dear Zippy,

I don't think I have mentioned this lately, but your writing skills are coming along nicely.

I know much of this is due to Winslow's guidance, particularly in terms of spelling. He has always been an excellent speller. So please share my praise with him.

Speaking of writing, I regret that I have to cut back on the number of letters I send to you in Baltimore. Pamela's mother has begun volunteering at the elementary school Pamela attended, and I have been helping her. She and I remained involved with Clarendon Elementary even after Pamela went to junior high, high school, and then college and grad school. (I know you found two stints at Puppy Kindergarten a bit excessive, not to mention your recent experience with agility training. But people go to school much, much longer. Pamela didn't seem to know when to stop.)

The schools in Cleveland have started cutting back on arts classes. This is a terrible thing. Pamela's mother fell in love with painting in elementary school, and Pamela fell in love with theater then, too. That led to Pamela's father and mother taking her to lots of plays and eventually to her becoming a theater critic and getting hired by the newspaper in Baltimore, where she met the cutest pup in Baltimore – you! That's how important arts education is.

The art teacher at Clarendon retired at the end of the school year. She had been Pamela's art teacher, and she and Pamela's mother kept in touch. Just before school started again, the art teacher learned that the school board was eliminating all art classes. Pamela's mother asked her if there was anything she could do.

Now, three or four afternoons a week, we go to the school, where I am proud to be Clarendon's unofficial, assistant after-school art teacher volunteer.

I hope you understand if you don't hear from me quite so often. Please know that I am thinking of you, but the students at Clarendon are my new project, just the way you are Pamela and Frank's project. Both projects are very, very important.

Love,
Grandma Vivienne

DeaR Grandma Vivienne,

Zippy is also working.

Zippy is still Pamela's A Number One research assiStant.

ZIppy is Researching ANNie.

Annie has a dog named SAndy.

Sandy is a rescue Dog like Zippy!!!

Pamela has a toy SANdy dog.

Pamela said it is for photO Shoot.

Zippy remembers Annie has a GUN!

Don't shoot SANdy dog!!!!

Zippy rescued ToY SANDy Dog.

Ran aroUnd the house wIth it.

Showed it The House.

RAN upstairs.

rAn downStairs.

SAVed toy Dog.

Pamela gave Zippy a biscuit to Drop toy Dog.

Nothing More said about shooting dog.

A Good Day of REsearch!!!

Love,

Zippy

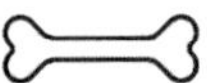

Dear GrandMA Vivienne,

OH, boy!!!

Oh, BoY!!!!!

Zippy is going into show business!

What is show businesS?

iS it like a dog show?

Zippy does not want to be in a dog shoW!

Zippy Wants to be an actresS!

Pamela interviews Actresses.

Zippy is going to be famous,

more famous than Sandy dog.

LOVe,

Zippy

Dear Grandma Vivienne,

There has been an interesting turn of events around here. As Zippy has told you, Pamela is writing about the musical "Annie," and Zippy has taken a great interest in Annie's canine co-star, Sandy. (She also thinks this is the same "Annie" as the one in "Annie Get Your Gun," but that's a different matter.)

One of Pamela's articles is about people who train dogs for Broadway shows. Besides the dog in "Annie," there's a whole raft of dogs in a new Broadway show called "The Will Rogers Follies." Pamela interviewed that show's trainer, too.

Pamela has been working from home lately, and she conducted this interview over the phone in the den. I happened to be dozing at her feet at the time. But when I repeatedly heard the word "dog," my ears perked up. I tuned into the interview rather late, but here's the part I overheard:

"You call your business 'Merry Mutts,' and I'm impressed by the fact that you use only rescue dogs. Why do you prefer rescue dogs?"

"You certainly have a cute troupe of pups. In fact, looking at the photo from 'Will Rogers Follies,' I can't help but notice that the little white one looks just like my own rescue dog, Zippy. The dogs you select must depend on the needs of each show. What are you looking for now?

"I see — another small white one. An understudy."

"Oh, 'underdog.'"

"Yes, I can send you Zippy's picture."

"Yes, she's a very good jumper — a high jumper. She's also high-spirited. Very lively."

"Yes, she gets along with other dogs."

"Well, I appreciate your interest and will definitely send you that photo. Thank you for a fascinating interview."

Zippy was also in the room during this conversation, and at the mention of her name, she launched into her running-in-circles routine with enough gusto to generate electricity for a small town.

After Pamela hung up, she patted Zippy on the head and said, "So, little girl, how would you like to be on Broadway? Who needs a show dog when you could have a show-business dog!"

As if this terpsichorean terrier doesn't have an elevated enough opinion of herself already! Not to mention that if performers who overact are said to chew the scenery, over-zealous Zippy will rip it to shreds.

Personally — or should I say, caninally? — I'm not sure what to make of Zippy's chance to be in the limelight, but at least it has distracted Pamela from her latest worries about the baby and about Frank. I don't know if he's still meeting with those nice people in the church basement each morning. Maybe he just hasn't taken me with him.

I have no doubt that you are having fun with the children in your art classes, but Zippy and I miss your letters and hope you will write again soon.

Yours,

Winslow

Cleveland Heights, Ohio
Friday, October 18, 1991

My dear Zippy,

I am sorry your show business career ended so abruptly - before it got started, actually. I can well appreciate the disappointment that led you to have a tiny accident on Pamela's shoe when she broke the news.

Now that some time has passed, I hope you can better appreciate Pamela's decision. As I am sure she tried to explain, when she heard back from Merry Mutts, they told her you looked perfect. It seems, however, that initially they neglected to tell her that they own all of their dogs. You would have had to live with Merry Mutts – permanently.

And, as much as Pamela and Frank wanted you to be a Broadway star, they were not willing to give you up. So, you will have to content yourself with being a star in Pamela and Frank's firmament. That's a fancy word for "sky," and it shines all the brighter because of you.

I am enclosing copies of some of the pictures the after-school art students have painted. We started with simple subjects, like flowers and trees. Then we asked the children what they would like to paint. It turns out almost all of them have pets, and most of those pets are dogs and cats. If they don't have a pet of their own, one of their relatives does.

Because they were so eager to talk about these pets, I went around the room and asked each student to share a pet story. Then they set about painting the pet's portrait. I think the pictures came out quite nicely.

Next week we will be working on the children's Halloween costumes. You probably don't remember last year's Halloween, because you were too young. Halloween grew out of a harvest festival. People would dress in costumes to ward off evil spirits. Now the holiday is celebrated by children dressing in costumes. They go door to door saying, "Trick or treat?" and getting candy at each house.

Although you would love trick or treating, I think Pamela and Frank have another important Halloween duty in mind for you. Pamela has gotten you your own costume, and I know you will do a good job.

Halloween is also close to the time of year Frank found you, so you have a lot to celebrate. Have fun and don't let all the ghouls and goblins scare you.

Love,
Grandma Vivienne

CHAPTER 10

Dear Grandma Vivienne,

Do NOT like costume!

Pamela says Zippy is an ANgel dog.

THis is true.

Pamela says Zippy is official trick-or-treat greeter.

PaMela puts wings on Zippy.

WIngs are on stretchy straps.

Legs get tangled in straps.

HALo is worse!!!

STRaps go around head.

Doorbell rings.

Doorbell rings againandagainandagain

Zippy barksandbarksandbarksandbarks.

This is Zippy's real job:

Protect and defend.

Zippy gets time out in crate.

NOT Fair.

Zippy is doing her job!!!

ZIPPy pretends bad costume is bath water.

Shake it off shake it off shakeshakeshake.

WINGs fall down below tummy.

Halo flops around.

Halo lands in front of mouth.

Zippy chews halo.

When Pamela opens crate she says

Next year you will be a devil dog.

NOT Fair!!!

LOVe,

Zippy the angel dog

Cleveland Heights, Ohio
Friday, November 15, 1991

My dear Zippy,

The sad account of your Halloween costume reminded me of something Pamela told me about her early childhood, long before I came along.

Pamela's mother gave her an angel doll. Pamela loved this doll. But the doll had an unusual feature. Its wings were tied on with a bow and could be removed. This must have been similar to the way your Halloween wings worked, but without the elastic.

When Pamela was good, the angel wore its wings. But if Pamela did something naughty, her mother took away the angel's wings. This upset Pamela tremendously. She could not understand why the angel had to be punished for something the angel didn't do.

One time, after Pamela did something especially naughty, her mother put the angel – without its wings – on top of the refrigerator. Pamela said she cried and cried because the angel couldn't fly down. Pamela's mother felt awful about upsetting her this way, so the next day, she sewed the angel's wings on permanently.

By dressing you in an angel costume, Pamela may have been trying to restore the angel's wings, all these years later.

On second thought, Pamela may not have been thinking about the angel doll at all when she bought your angel costume. She probably was just thinking about what an angel you are. That's definitely the way I think of you.

So, do not fear, dear Zippy. Even if you wind up with horns and a pitchfork next Halloween, you will always be an angel dog to me.

Love,
Grandma Vivienne

Dear Grandma Vivienne,

Zippy and Winslow coming to Cleveland for Turkey DAY!

CAN't wait!!!

Ride in car.

Save turkey liver for me.

Zippy deserves turkey liver.

Zippy is an angel dog.

See you soon!

Yippeee!!!!!

Love,

Zippy

Dear Grandma Vivienne,

NO trip to Cleveland.

Why not???

Pamela in bed.

FRAnk brings food on tray.

Zippy tries to be nursing terrier.

Jumps on bed when tray is on bed.

Zippy, get away from that tray.

Zippy, get off the bed. Now!

Frank is gone.

For a long time.

Winslow waits at the door.

No happiness here.

Why not?

Love,

Zippy

Cleveland Heights, Ohio
Tuesday, December 3, 1991

My dear Zippy,

I am very grateful for your letter. Pamela keeps telling me everything is fine. But clearly it is not, particularly if Frank is not there. I called Pamela as soon as I read what you wrote.

Pamela's mother is flying to Baltimore tomorrow. Although she will probably get there before this letter reaches you, I want to try to explain what has happened.

Pamela had a doctor's appointment a few days before Thanksgiving. At the appointment, the doctor took a picture of the baby – the people puppy I said was coming to live with you.

The people puppy was supposed to be moving, but it had stopped doing so. Zippy, it is difficult for me to write this, but there is not going to be a people puppy.

The doctor told Pamela that this happens sometimes, seemingly without cause. Pamela sounded surprisingly calm when she talked to me about this. But your letter convinced me that things are not calm.

I will try to put all of this another way that may be easier for you to take in. Years ago, Pamela's father and mother had a sweet dog named Morsels, who was expecting puppies. When the puppies arrived, however, they did not move and had to be taken away. Morsels wandered around the house for days looking for her puppies.

As the doctor told Pamela, there are times in life when sad things happen for no apparent reason. It can be especially helpful to have a dog like you around at these times. Pamela may not feel like playing with you. She may try to shoo you away. But if you stay by her side – quietly – you will be more welcome than you know.

Keep this letter and, if you get confused about what happened, read it over. I hope it will help.

Love,
Grandma Vivienne

Dear Grandma Vivienne,

Pamela was happy her mother was here.

Zippy was happy, too.

Zippy had fun with Pamela's mother.

Fun throwing tennis balls.

Fun baking HAnukkah biscuits.

Biscuits shaped like BAD BAD BAD dreidel.

Bad dreidel biscuits taste good!!!

Zippy is working on her typing.

The quick brown DOG jumps over the lazy fox.

Frank came home.

Zippy watched Pamela's mother on the front porch with Frank.

Pamela said her mother and Frank had words.

What does that mean???

Zippy writes lots of words.

Everything is back to normal here.

Pamela is back at work.

Frank is back at work.

Zippy and Winslow home ALL DAY.

No one talks about people puppy.

Zippy thinks Pamela misses people puppy.

LOOVE oops Love,

Zippy

Cleveland Heights, Ohio
Wednesday, December 18, 1991

My dear Zippy,

Pamela's mother says you have developed into

an excellent nursing terrier. She also told me she tried not to show it, but she was upset about circumstances there, and you were a cheering presence for her as well as for Pamela.

I must say, your typing has become quite proficient (that means quite good). You just have to focus on being a bit less enthusiastic about the capital letters key. (By the way, the practice sentence that uses all of the letters on the keyboard is: "The quick brown fox jumps over the lazy dog," not "the quick brown dog" and "the lazy fox." But I think you know that.)

We have only two days of school left before the children's Christmas vacation, but being with you and Winslow gave Pamela's mother lots of ideas for holiday art projects. We had the children make ornaments related to their pets. Some made dog biscuit-shaped ornaments. Some made ornaments with miniature pictures of the pets.

My favorite was a pair of ornaments made by a talented 4th grader. One ornament was a miniature red fire hydrant. The other was a male dog with its leg raised. Very funny!

I have enclosed the recipe for the holiday biscuits Pamela's mother made in Baltimore, in case Pamela or Frank want to make them for you and Winslow. I trust you didn't mind my tasting one. I thought they were so yummy, I am thinking of making a batch for my New Year's Day open house – and serving them to people!

I hope you have a joyful New Year's Eve – your second New Year's! I understand that you and Pamela and Frank have been invited to a party at Janet's house. I am sure you will be on your best behavior in the presence of your former trainer. Make her proud!

Love,
Grandma Vivienne

Holiday Dog Biscuits

- 2 ½ cups flour
- ¾ cup dry milk
- 1 egg, beaten
- ½ cup vegetable oil
- 2 chicken bouillon cubes dissolved in ¾ cup boiling water
- 2 tablespoons grated parmesan cheese

Preheat oven to 300 degrees. Spray cookie sheet with cooking spray. Mix flour, egg, oil, dry milk, and parmesan cheese. Add cooled chicken broth and continue mixing. Knead dough, then roll out. Use Hanukkah, Christmas, or Valentine cookie cutters to make holiday-shaped biscuits. Bake for 35-40 minutes. (NOTE: Blue, red, or green food coloring can be added to the mixed ingredients, but this is purely to please the dogs' owner; the dogs will not notice.)

CHAPTER 11

Dear Grandma Vivienne,

President Bush threw up in Japan!

Zippy loves watching this on TV.

It is on TV over and over.

President Bush hates broccoli.

Zippy hates broccoli.

Frank put some in Zippy's dish once.

YUck!

President Bush has a dog named Millie who wrote a book.

Zippy likes Millie.

Zippy likes President BUsh.

Pamela and Frank do not like President Bush.

Why?

Janet's New Year's party was fun.

Pamela had fun.

Frank had fun.

Zippy had fun.

Janet made treats for dogs.

Janet put people treats out of reach of dogs.

Zippy was disappointed but liked dog treats.

Pamela asked Janet to send you recipes.

Have to go now.

News is on TV.

Maybe see PResident throw up again.

Love,

Zippy

Cleveland Heights, Ohio
Friday, January 24, 1992

My dear Zippy,

I am glad to get your happy report about Janet's New Year's party, and especially glad that Pamela and Frank had fun. I am also glad to see that you are taking an interest in politics. I can understand why you like Millie, the presidental dog. I have ordered you a copy of "Millie's Book: As Dictated to Barbara Bush." It is being mailed directly to you.

There is a long tradition of presidential dogs, going all the way back to the first president, George Washington. Before Richard Nixon was elected president, he gave a famous speech about a dog named Checkers, who was a gift to his daughters.

Another president, Harry Truman, once said: "You want a friend in Washington? Get a dog." But he gave away his Cocker Spaniel, Feller, so I guess he didn't want any friends. (Hmmm... maybe I shouldn't have mentioned Feller. Sometimes people in Washington make errors in judgment. Do not let that bother you, dear Zippy.)

Pamela's mother particularly admired a presidential dog named Fala, a Scottish Terrier who belonged to President Franklin Roosevelt. This was in the 1940s, when men wore wide silk ties. Hand-painted ties were especially fashionable. Pamela's mother painted a portrait of Fala on a tie and mailed it to the president.

President Roosevelt suffered from a disease called polio, and he started a charity called the March of Dimes to raise money to combat polio. Pamela's mother wrote the name "Fala" in dimes on the outside of the tie box. President Roosevelt wrote her a thank-you note! She still has the note. She can show it to you the next time you come to visit.

As to why Pamela and Frank do not like President Bush, a lot has to do with the invasion of Iraq last year. You were still a puppy at the time, and you were upset by the explosions on the TV news.

But that is enough history for one letter. The important thing to know is that there have been some wonderful dogs in the White House, and I am sure they have been a great source of joy and support to America's presidents, just as you are a great source of joy and support to Pamela and Frank.

Love,
Grandma Vivienne

Dear Grandma Vivienne,

Zippy loves Millie's Book!

Millie meets the Queen of England.

Millie attends important meetings in the Oval Office.

Millie digs up tulips.

Millie plays with tennis balls.

Millie has puppies.

Something happened with Pamela.

Maybe about the missing people puppy.

Pamela was wrapping a present.

She said it was for a baby shower.

Zippy didn't know babies have to take showers.

Zippy hates being a wet dog.

Zippy feels very sorry for wet soapy babies.

Zippy was helping wrap the gift.

Pamela pushed the gift away and started crying.

Pamela hugged Zippy and cried some more.

Zippy jumped on table and pulled ribbon.

Zippy pulled and pulled.

Pamela yelled Bad Dog.

Zippy jumped down and ran in circles.

Got tangled in ribbon.

Pamela laughed.

Pamela picked up Zippy.

UNtangled Zippy.

Said Zippy is a good dog.

Zippy is going to write a letter to Millie.

Love,

Zippy

Mildred Kerr Bush
The White House
Washington, D.C.

Dear Millie,

Zippy read your book.

Very good book.

Lots of pictures.

Zippy does many things Millie does.

Zippy chases tennis balls.

Zippy digs up flowers.

Zippy goes to important meetings.

Zippy does not dictate her letters.

Zippy types letters herself.

Zippy could type letters for Millie.

Could be Official Secretary to Presidential Dog.

Please let Zippy know if position is open.

Sincerely,

Zippy

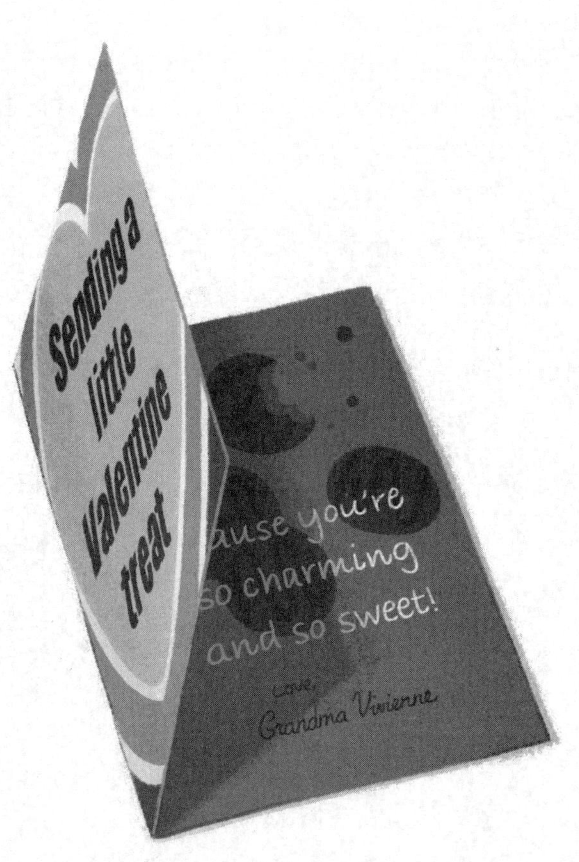

Dear Zippy and Winslow,

This card originally came with a small packet of candy conversation hearts inside. Remembering, however, what happened to Zippy with last year's Valentine candy, I have replaced the conversation hearts with two heart-shaped dog biscuits – one for each of you.

I bought these at a fancy pet store here in Cleveland. I am not sure what the icing is made of, but Pamela's mother and I are going to do some experiments to see if we can duplicate it.

Have a happy Hearts' Day. Give Pamela and Frank lots of love and affection. And do not eat any candy!

Love,
Grandma Vivienne

Dear Grandma Vivienne,

Zippy is angry at Millie.

Millie dictates book.

Millie does not even dictate letter to Zippy!!!

Sends picture from book cover.

Pamela says Millie is a Republican dog.

A Democratic dog would have written.

What does that mean?

Millie is not Zippy's friend.

Millie is a Bad Dog.

Love,

ZZippy

Cleveland Heights, Ohio
Friday, March 6, 1992

My dear Zippy,

I completely understand your indignation over the form letter and stock photo you received from Millie Bush. You would think that a dog raised in the White House would have better manners. Millie clearly did not have the advantage of attending a puppy charm school on the level of Janet's. Pamela may be correct about the Republican influence; a Democrat would have been more open-minded.

I will attempt a brief explanation of America's two-party political system. First, I am sorry to say that these are not parties with cake and games. Wait. Let me correct that. Sometimes there is cake and there are definitely games, but not the kind you are accustomed to playing (no fetch, no squeak toys, no tennis balls).

I will start again. These parties have to do with political beliefs and voting for the candidate who best represents the voter's beliefs. American citizens can register with either party (or no party). Pamela's mother is a registered Democrat. So is Frank. Pamela is not registered with either party because, as a newspaper writer, she does not want to be seen as favoring one party over the other.

Dogs, regrettably, cannot register and cannot vote. Grandma Vivienne cannot register, either. At heart, I suspect you are a Democrat, but not a Yellow or Blue Dog Democrat. This is not just because you are a white dog; "yellow" and "blue" do not refer to the color of a dog's coat, but more to different philosophical—

Oh, my, I was trying to make a joke, but explaining it is too complicated. So, hoping you understand at least some of my attempted civics lesson, that will be all for now.

I think I had more to tell you – not about political parties – but all of this political talk has completely distracted me. All politics aside, I am certain that you are a party animal, and that's what counts.

Love,
Grandma Vivienne

P.S. I just remembered what I intended to write about and it is very important. Pamela and Frank are taking a vacation to an island called Bermuda. A vacation is a happy event, but they are taking this trip to help get over the sad loss of the people puppy, who was supposed to arrive next month. You and Winslow will be going to a new camp, and I do not want to hear a single complaint this time. Pamela has thoroughly investigated this camp. It has lots of fun activities. So have a good time and, if you get a chance, drop me a line letting me know how much you are enjoying yourself.

Dear Grandma Vivienne,

Oh, no!

Suitcases in the bedroom.

Suitcases are bad.

Zippy pushed bad suitcases off the bed.

Clothes on the floor.

Zippy in time out.

Pamela and Frank are leaving soon.

Zippy and Winslow are going to camp soon.

Save Zippy and Winslow!!!

Love,

Zippy

Deear Grandma Vivienne,

New camp is bad!!!

Chihuahua nipping at Zippy during play timee.

Zippy chaseeed the Chihuahua into a corneeer.

Chihuahua whineed and barkeeed.

Zippy got timee out.

Unfair!!! Unfair!!! Unfair!!!

Zippy found old typeewriteeeer.

Leetteeeer eeeeee brokeeeen.

Good food at camp.

Chihuahua is going homeeee.

Loveeeee,

Zippy

Cleveland Heights, Ohio
Wednesday, March 25, 1992

My dear Zippy,

I am glad you survived canine camp despite the rocky start with the Chihuahua. I am actually quite proud of your behavior. A less disciplined dog would have growled or snapped at the irritating creature. I understand that you merely gave chase and held the offender at bay. Wise strategy!

I have a development to share that should interest you. When Pamela and Frank arrived in Bermuda, they had to go through something called "Customs." This is a procedure in which officials find out why you are entering the country and whether you are carrying any contraband.

"Contraband" refers to things brought into a country illegally. Usually these are things like guns or drugs. But wait until you hear what is contraband in Bermuda!

Pamela told me that she and Frank had to wait in a long line to go through Customs. She said Frank got very perturbed – that's similar to the way you feel when your dinner is taking too long and you start barking.

Pamela, however, passed the time reading the boring Customs document in detail. Right there on the document, it said that it is illegal to bring a dog into Bermuda! Apparently, a dog must be quarantined for six months – that's a really long time-out – to make sure the animal is healthy.

This got Pamela thinking – what if she wanted to bring Zippy to Bermuda? How could she sneak you in?

Being a writer, Pamela decided this would make a good children's book. She began writing "Zippy Goes to Bermuda" on the days Frank was off deep-sea fishing.

She asked her mother to do the illustrations. But her mother said she hasn't painted pictures of dogs in years, and nowadays she doesn't really feel up to it. So, I offered to do the illustrations myself! And what better subject could there be than Zippy?

Meanwhile, I am sure preparations are underway for your upcoming birthday, and I am also sure you can count on cake. At two years old, you will be an adult dog – an exciting milestone.

Love,
Grandma Vivienne

CHAPTER 12

Love and joy and Milk-Bones, too!
These are what I wish for you
As you reach the age of two.
Happy 2nd Birthday!
Love,
Grandma Vivienne

<u>Enclosed note</u>: As your gift, Zippy, I am sending this recipe for a canine birthday cake, which I hope Pamela and Frank will bake for you.

ZIPPY's BIRTHDAY CAKE

- 1 cup whole wheat flour
- 1 teaspoon baking soda
- ⅓ cup honey
- ¼ cup vegetable oil
- ¼ cup natural peanut butter
- 1 cup shredded carrots
- 1 egg
- softened cream cheese

Preheat oven to 350 degrees. Combine dry ingredients. Stir in wet ingredients and shredded carrots. Grease a small loaf pan and a tin for four muffins. Pour in batter. Bake for 30 minutes. After cooled, arrange in shape of dog bone: loaf cake in middle, two muffins on each end. Frost with thin layer of softened cream cheese.

Dear Grandma Vivienne,

Zippy's Birthday Cake is scrumptious!!!

Winslow helped Zippy with that word.

Winslow also helped eat the cake.

Zippy did not need that help.

Frank is excited about new ballpark.

Went to new ballpark.

Did not take Zippy.

Zippy loves balls.

Zippy loves parks.

Frank said Cleveland beat Baltimore.

Why did Cleveland and Baltimore fight?

Zippy likes Cleveland and Baltimore.

Frank came home and threw his cap at the wall.

Zippy fetched the cap.

Brought it to Frank.

Zippy could not get Frank to throw the cap again.

Frank grabbed the cap and stomped upstairs.

What did Zippy do wrong?

Zippy does not want to go to the ballpark.

Love,

Zippy

Cleveland Heights, Ohio
Saturday, April 11, 1992

My dear Zippy,

Let me begin by assuring you that Baltimore did not fight Cleveland. Each city has sports teams, and the teams of one city play games against the teams of another. Baltimore's team and Cleveland's team were playing a baseball game and Cleveland's team won.

Baseball is kind of like a game of fetch, but it's played with a wooden bat in a ballpark. One player throws the ball and another player hits it with the bat and runs – a little like you catching a ball and running in circles with it.

The important thing is that Baltimore and Cleveland get along just fine. They have no hard feelings. Their teams merely compete in professional sports.

And Zippy, you did not do anything wrong. Do not worry. Pamela has told me that Frank tends to get too involved with baseball games. Maybe you have seen him yelling at the TV. At the ballpark, he may have had too many refreshments, which could have made him even more upset when Baltimore lost.

Zippy, I am concerned about how much you worry. You have always had a tendency to worry, but it seems to be increasing. You may have picked this up from Pamela. (Her father often commented that, over time, dogs begin to resemble their owners.) Worrying is not a productive trait. It does not help Pamela, and it does not help you. You are, by nature, a cheerful creature, and if you strive to be more carefree, both you and Pamela will benefit.

Speaking of cheerful distractions, Pamela sent me the first chapter of "Zippy Goes to Bermuda," and I have enclosed it here. The dog in the book sounds like a very plucky character, just like you. Feel free to share these pages with Winslow. I am eager to know what you both think.

Love,
Grandma Vivienne

ZIPPY GOES TO BERMUDA
Chapter One

Bonnie Bright lived with her parents and her dog Zippy in a small Midwestern town on a beautiful lake. In the summer, Bonnie Bright and Zippy would swim in the lake and go boating on the lake and sometimes they would catch fish in the lake.

But in the winter, it was very, very cold living near the lake. The winds would whip up the snow in great whirls of flakes. If Zippy – who was a fluffy white terrier – didn't wear her pink sweater, she would almost disappear in the clouds of white snow.

One winter it was so cold and so icy, Bonnie Bright and Zippy rarely got to play outside. Bonnie's parents promised that before winter was over, they would take her to a warm, sunny island called Bermuda, where they could all thaw out.

So, one day in early March, Bonnie Bright packed a suitcase full of swimsuits and shorts and sundresses and sandals. Then she picked out some books and puzzles and her favorite doll and put them in her backpack to take on the plane.

When she got in her parents' car to go to the airport, Bonnie noticed that her backpack was heavier than she expected, but she didn't think much about it. The weather was so snowy and icy and cold, Bonnie couldn't wait to get to sunny Bermuda.

After the plane took off, Bonnie Bright began opening her backpack to take out a book. Lo and behold, a shiny nose poked out and started sniffing! Bonnie opened the backpack some more and a pair of dark eyes looked up at her. Zippy had stowed away in the backpack!

Luckily, no one noticed. Bonnie Bright's parents were busy reading magazines and the flight attendants were busy serving drinks to other passengers. Bonnie broke into a grin and gave Zippy a few pats on the head. Then she made a soft "shushing" sound and gently eased the dog's head back into the bag. This time, though, she left a small opening to give the dog more air. Bonnie spent the rest of the flight daydreaming about the fun she and Zippy were going to have in Bermuda.

After the plane landed, Bonnie Bright and her parents found themselves in a long line in a large room with a sign that said: "Customs." Everyone was handed a list of Customs

Regulations. Because there was nothing else to do, Bonnie began reading the list.

"No firearms, no illicit drugs, no fresh fruit, no fresh vegetables, no dogs..." No dogs! Bonnie Bright read that again. "All dogs entering Bermuda will be quarantined for a period of six months to ensure that rabies and other canine-born diseases are not brought onto the island."

Zippy had been very quiet during the flight, so Bonnie Bright was sure she could sneak the dog past Customs. But as the line crept closer to the Customs agents, she noticed that they were opening many of the bags and examining the contents.

Nervously, Bonnie Bright began watching the people in the other lines. There were lots of children and none of them seemed nervous. Clearly, it was important not to seem nervous. Some of the children were holding their parents' hands. Some were carrying dolls or stuffed animals — teddy bears, sock monkeys and, wait, could that be a stuffed dog?

That was it! As Bonnie Bright and her parents approached the front of the line, Bonnie opened her backpack. She took out her doll and let it dangle from her left hand. Then, whispering, "Stay still!" to Zippy, she lifted the dog out and gently placed the animal under her right arm. She assumed an air of confidence as she and her family walked up to the Customs agent. She smiled, as if to say, "See how helpful I am — I've opened my backpack for you to inspect. I've even taken out some of my toys."

At that moment, another Customs official came over. "Oh, no!" Bonnie thought. "We've been found out!" Instead, without a word, the official stepped around the Bright family and presented their agent with a stack of papers. The agent was rifling through the papers when Bonnie's mother handed him their passports. He looked at the passports ever so briefly, stamped them, and waved the Bright family along, barely noticing the little girl and her "stuffed" dog.

And just like that, Zippy was in Bermuda!

Dear Grandma Vivienne,

Zippy Goes to Bermuda is the best book Zippy has ever read!

Much better than Millie's Book!

Who is Bonnie Bright???

Zippy does not know Bonnie Bright.

Zippy does not live in a small midwestern town.

Zippy does not go fishing.

Book is not true.

But Zippy likes the book.

All dogs would like Zippy Goes to Bermuda.

Zippy is ready to pose for illustrations.

Love,

Zippy

“Zippy Goes to Bermuda,” Chapter One,
reviewed by Winslow

“Zippy Goes to Bermuda” (Chapter One) is built on a highly amusing premise that is certain to please children and their parents as well. Setting a curious canine loose in a foreign land unlatches the gate to all kinds of intriguing adventures. I am eager to read more.

This reviewer, however, feels obligated to mention two disturbing elements that surface in the first chapter. One: Zippy gains entry to Bermuda through a deceptive — actually illegal — stratagem. This could set the wrong example for impressionable children.

Two: Having Zippy pose as a stuffed animal suggests that dogs are mere inanimate playthings. Anyone with any knowledge of dogs will tell you that dogs are serious animals who fulfill the very important roles of providing companionship, comfort, and countless hours of lively — as in “alive” — entertainment to humans.

These objections aside, “Zippy Goes to Bermuda” has great potential. Illustrations can only enhance the book’s appeal. I can picture Zippy boating on the lake at home, poking her nose out of the backpack on the plane, and yes, dare I say it, passing herself off as a stuffed dog at Customs.

Even at this early stage, “Zippy Goes to Bermuda” shows signs of being the next “Pokey Little Puppy.” I do have one suggestion, however. Zippy's adventures would surely benefit from a canine sidekick. A Boston Terrier, for example, would add gravitas and wisdom to the whippersnapper's shenanigans.

Your devoted and astute critic,

Winslow

P.S. The Bermuda vacation appears to have had a salutary effect on Pamela and Frank. They came home much more relaxed, and working on "Zippy Goes to Bermuda" seems to be extending that effect for Pamela. Several times I have caught her chuckling at the typewriter. Who would have thought that our over-active, tizzy of a Zippy would turn out to be a literary muse? Certainly not this seasoned and sedate Boston Terrier.

P.P.S. Your observation that Zippy is a worrier is absolutely correct. Most members of my species live in the moment. Not Zippy. When she grabs onto a notion, she clings to it with, as the phrase goes, dogged determination.

I do my level-headed best — and I am nothing if not level-headed — to assuage her worries. Failing that, I feel there may be therapeutic value in allowing her to put her worries in writing. Of course, the animal has no sense of proportion. For her, not being able to find a tennis ball is as distressing as not being able to find Frank; either one can result in a round of frenzied tail-chasing.

Ah, well. I guess it is my fate to cope with the whims of this perpetually impatient pup. In dog years, she is now a teenager. In people years, she's a toddler. I don't know which is worse.

Cleveland Heights, Ohio
Wednesday, May 6, 1992

Dear Zippy and Winslow,

I heartily agree with your favorable responses to Pamela's first chapter. And Zippy, though we cannot know how many dogs will read this book, you make a valid point that they would enjoy it if they did.

Zippy, you expressed confusion about the character of Bonnie Bright. Although you are the heroine – the star – of "Zippy Goes to Bermuda," it is a work of fiction. That means it is an imaginary, "make-believe" story. For instance, Zippy, you have never been to Bermuda in real life. The story merely imagines would what happen if you tried to go. Similarly, Bonnie Bright is an imaginary, "make-believe" character.

Winslow, I respect your comment that dogs are serious animals. You yourself are a very serious dog. Nor can I argue with the fact that dogs provide comfort and companionship. But in this case, I think you are taking matters <u>too</u> seriously. A bit of mischief can be humorous, and because a dog is the star of the story, I am sure she will be portrayed in a positive light.

As to your suggestion that Zippy have a Boston Terrier sidekick, sneaking two dogs into Bermuda would be an even less likely premise, but I will ask Pamela to consider it. Perhaps Zippy could meet up with a Boston Terrier who lives in Bermuda…

I want to mention one other thing. This Sunday is a holiday called Mother's Day. It may be difficult for Pamela and Frank this year. Winslow, I know you will be, as ever, a soothing presence. And Zippy, just be your playful self, but do follow Winslow's laid-back example.

Your encouraging reactions to "Zippy Goes to Bermuda" – as well as my desire to give Pamela something else to focus on – prompted me to do some preliminary sketches of Zippy. I have sent these to Pamela. If she likes them, I hope she will show them to you.

I will have more time to devote to the illustrations when the school year is over. And Zippy, much as I appreciate your offer to pose, it will not be necessary. I have plenty of photographs, and I am certain that I can capture your exuberant spirit.

Also, rest assured, Zippy and Winslow, that I will share all of your insights with Pamela. I know she will appreciate them. After all, your perspective is invaluable.

Your grateful and loving,
Grandma Vivienne

CHAPTER 13

Dear Grandma Vivienne,

Cheese omelets on Sundays.

Zippy and Winslow get some cheese omelet.

Yummy.

Omelets with kibble and cheese would be better.

Grandma Vivienne must write a recipe.

Pamela held Zippy in her lap and called Pamela's mom.

Pamela said happy Mother's Day.

Zippy licked Pamela's face.

Salty.

Pamela and Frank are going to a movie.

Frank went out to get something from his car.

Frank did not come back.

Pamela and Frank did not go to the movie.

Pamela on the telephone.

Pamela vacuuming, more vacuuming, more vacuuming.

Zippy hates vacuum!!!

Zippy stayed near Pamela.

Zippy get out from underfoot!

Zippy why are you always underfoot?

Zippy you need a timeout.

More vacuuming.

No Frank.

Where is Frank?

Is Zippy a bad dog?

Too much vacuuming.

Love,

Zippy

Cleveland Heights, Ohio
Saturday, May 16, 1992

My dear Zippy,

You know how fond you are of chocolate? You may not remember this, but chocolate makes you very sick. Last year, you ended up at the vet after you ate all of Pamela's Valentine's Day candy.

I am bringing up this unfortunate incident to explain what happened to Frank. Frank also likes to overdo something, but it is not candy. It is alcohol. Just as you could not stop eating the chocolate candy, he cannot stop drinking alcohol, and it makes him sick.

You might say that you have a chocolate problem and he has an alcohol problem. You went to the vet when you ate too much chocolate. Frank is also at a hospital. He will be away for a while, but then he will come home.

Both of Frank's parents had the same problem he does, and sometimes these things are passed on from parent to child. Although I compared your problem to Frank's, I want you to understand that you have <u>nothing</u> to do with his problem. Dogs do not pass problems like this on to people.

You are happiness itself. I am sure that when Frank is better and comes home, he will be very happy to see you again.

While Frank is away, however, you have to be an especially supportive dog for Pamela. I know you can do this. If she loses patience with you at times, try not to let it bother you. Pamela is going through another difficult period and may over-react to some of your, well, enthusiasm.

I am sorry to have written such a serious letter, but I wanted to reassure you that you are in no way to blame for what Frank is going through. You are a very good dog. You have always been a very good dog. And, as your devoted grandma, I know you will continue to be a very good dog. In fact, you can do no wrong in my eyes. So, keep up the good work.

Love,
Grandma Vivienne

P.S. To try to cheer you up, I have enclosed one of my sketches for "Zippy Goes to Bermuda." I hope you like it.

Dear Grandma Vivienne,

Zippy and Pamela are reading books together!

We are reading Co-Dependent No More and Courage to Change and AA's Big Book.

Too many books!

No pictures in these books.

No dogs in these books.

Zippy sits on Pamela's lap and we read and read and read and read.

We read all about twelve steps but we do not take any steps.

No walks.

No fetch.

Zippy does not whine.

Zippy wanders in the backyard.

Zippy misses walks.

Zippy misses Frank.

Love,

Zippy

P.S. Zippy loves Grandma Vivienne's drawing!

Zippy wags her tail in the drawing.

Zippy is wagging her tail now.

Cleveland Heights, Ohio
Wednesday, June 10, 1992

My dear Zippy,

You have written your first postscript! I am very proud of you. You are becoming quite a literate dog.

I understand your objections to the amount of reading that Pamela is doing. But you must remember that she loves research. If Frank's therapist suggests that she read three books, she will read six.

I am sure you also remember that Frank has called you Pamela's "research assistant." If she wants you to read these books along with her, then that is your job, even if the books are not as much fun as "Zippy Goes to Bermuda."

Now that Frank is out of the hospital, I think Pamela will get back to "Zippy Goes to Bermuda." I hope so, anyway, because I enjoy doing the drawings. Maybe I can draw Zippy getting so excited, she does an unexpected back flip. That's what Pamela said you did when you saw Frank. I am sure he was just as glad to see you, even if he did not do a back flip.

You are a great source of positive energy to Pamela and Frank — and to me. Your response to my sketch inspired a year-end assignment for the art students at Clarendon Elementary School. Each child has to make three to five drawings or paintings of a dog or cat. One ambitious fourth grader has already completed three drawings of her family's Poodle. I will take the best one to the library and Xerox it for you.

I want to get this in today's mail, so I am going to stop writing and head to the library and then the post office.

Love,
Grandma Vivienne

Dear Grandma Vivienne,

Drawing of Poodle is okay.

Not great art like your drawing of Zippy.

Drawing of Zippy is on the refrigerator.

Zippy looks at it all the time.

Seeing it makes Zippy an even happier dog.

Frank and Pamela are also happy.

Frank takes Zippy on long walks.

Frank takes Zippy to the park.

Frank and Pamela go to meetings.

Frank and Pamela talk about the meetings.

Zippy has not met anyone.

Pamela says her mother is coming here for the holiday and fireworks.

Zippy is not afraid of fireworks any more.

But Zippy does not like fireworks.

Love,

Zippy

Cleveland Heights, Ohio
Friday, July 10, 1992

My dear Zippy,

I am relieved that fireworks no longer terrify you and that you no longer try to leap up and catch them. In short, I am glad that you no longer become hysterical.

From what I heard, you also helped calm Pamela and her mother down when Frank not only failed to show up for their backyard cookout, but stayed away most of the night. Pamela said that although they were warned this could happen, they were not expecting it, and certainly not so soon.

Zippy, I realize I am addressing you as an adult dog. In terms of age, of course, you are almost an adult. Plus, the composure you now show in trying circumstances makes me feel that you have become a mature animal. You are still a playful pup – and I hope you always will be – but your sweet nature also has a beneficial effect on those around you.

Did you know that there are dogs called Therapy Dogs? They provide comfort and ease anxiety in humans. Some go to hospitals and cheer up sick children. Others go to nursing homes and rekindle the love the residents felt for dogs they had long ago.

Therapy dogs have special training, but you have already proved to be an excellent Nursing Terrier, and now I think you also show signs of being an excellent Therapy Dog, but one, admittedly, that is self-taught.

I know Pamela's mother enjoyed her one-on-one time with you. She considered staying longer, but decided that Pamela and Frank needed to work on some things themselves – with your able help, of course. I do hope everything is settling down there. Pamela's mother and I are considering going to a meeting or two ourselves.

Love,
Grandma Vivienne

CHAPTER 14

Dear Grandma Vivienne,

Pamela and Frank and Winslow and Zippy are going to the beach!

We are going to Dewey Beach.

Is Dewey Beach near Bermuda?

Zippy is afraid of Customs agents.

Pamela says dogs can go to Dewey Beach.

Zippy will dig in the sand!

Zippy will ride in the car.

Zippy will stay in a hotel.

Zippy is a mature, adult dog.

Zippy will go to the beach!

Love,

Zippy

Cleveland Heights, Ohio
Thursday, August 6, 1992

My dear Zippy,

I am delighted that Pamela and Frank are going on a mini-vacation and taking you and Winslow with them. I think this is just the break that all of you need.

Have no fear. Dewey Beach is not near Bermuda, and there are no Customs agents. Even so, very few beaches anywhere allow dogs, so this will be a real treat. I am sure you are going to have a terrific time.

I hope you like the miniature beach ball I got you. Beach balls for people are usually inflatable, but I was afraid you might puncture one of those. So I was pleased to find this hard rubber beach ball dog toy.

As you will see, the ball will float in the ocean. It will put a whole new spin on your favorite game – fetch.

Have fun at Dewey Beach and don't let your cute pink tummy get sunburned!

Love,
Grandma Vivienne

Dear Grandma Vivienne,

Pamela and Frank and Winslow and Zippy are back home.

Hotel was fun.

Sand was fun.

Waves were not fun!

Water soaks Zippy.

Zippy barks.

Water goes away.

Water comes back.

Soaks Zippy again.

Zippy barks louder.

Water goes away.

Water comes back.

Again and again and again.

Bad water!

Pamela and Frank laugh.

Zippy does not think this is funny.

Pamela and Frank run in the waves.

Frank throws Zippy's beach ball into the waves.

Zippy does not fetch the ball.

Pamela and Frank play with Zippy's beach ball in the water.

Pamela and Frank do not act like mature adults.

Zippy is sticky with salt.

Zippy is sticky with sand.

Pamela soaks Zippy with the hose.

More water!!!

Not fun.

Love,

Zippy

Cleveland Heights, Ohio
Wednesday, September 2, 1992

My dear Zippy,

Clearly, you are not a water dog. And although you thought Pamela and Frank behaved immaturely – I suspect you thought this partly because they were using your ball – I am so happy to have an account of them having fun.

An exciting, unexpected development has occurred, and I have you and especially Winslow to thank for it. A few days ago, when Pamela's mother was at the supermarket, she ran into the publisher who published her series of cookbooks – "The Art of Appetizers," "The Art of Entrees," and "The Art of Desserts."

The publisher asked if Pamela's mother was working on any new cookbooks, and Pamela's mother jokingly said the only new recipes coming out of her kitchen these days were for dog biscuits!

Pamela's mother may not take these recipes seriously, but I do, and so did the publisher. He called later that afternoon to discuss a cookbook of recipes for dogs! Pamela's mother scoffed, but fortunately she handed me the phone.

And guess what? I am going to write almost the entire cookbook! I will be what is called a "ghost writer." That does not mean I am an actual ghost, but it does mean my name will not be on the book. So it goes.

I know Winslow thought this cookbook was a possibility from the start. You both have been inspirational! So, I guess I will have to come up with more recipes…

Right now, however, another school year is about to start, and Grandma Vivienne is looking forward to getting back to her young art students. Who knows? Maybe some of them could be cookbook illustrators!

Love to my two canine muses & taste testers,
Grandma Vivienne

Dear Grandma Vivienne,

Recipes! Recipes! Recipes!

Zippy is already testing.

Frank eats a meatloaf sandwich.

Doorbell rings.

Frank leaves the sandwich.

Zippy does a taste test.

Meatloaf yummy.

Bread with mustard is not yummy.

Leave that on the plate.

Onion is also not yummy.

Chew the onion into small pieces.

Spit the pieces on the floor.

Frank is not pleased.

Frank does not understand the importance of taste testing.

Frank yells at Zippy.

Frank laughs at Zippy.

Zippy is an excellent taste tester!

Love,

Zippy

Cleveland Heights, Ohio
Friday, September 25, 1992

My dear Zippy,

Thank you for taking your taste-testing duties to heart (perhaps I should say, "to tummy"). Meatloaf for dogs is a great idea!

Here is the recipe I have come up with (as you will see, it does not include mustard or onions):

- 2 cups ground beef, turkey, and veal
- 2 cups chopped carrots, parboiled potatoes, and peas
- 1 cup wheat germ
- 2 large eggs

Mix ingredients thoroughly. Bake in loaf pan for one hour at 350 degrees.

This makes a lot, so you will have plenty to share with Winslow. You can even share some with Pamela and Frank.

Pamela's mother and I have a nice group of art students this semester. Art is brand new to some of them, but a few took lessons over the summer.

One first-grader paints only in purple because that is her favorite color. So far she has painted a purple cat, a purple tree, and a purple school. I told her she is following a grand tradition: Picasso was one of the most famous painters in the world, and he had a blue period and a rose period. Put those together and you get a purple period.

One boy, however, draws only pictures of guns. This is troubling. Yesterday he picked up one of his gun pictures and pretended to shoot some of the other students. I am not sure how to handle this. I probably will talk to the school psychologist. (That's like a vet who specializes in what patients are thinking.)

But I should not trouble you with such things. I am eager to know how you and Winslow like the meatloaf.

Love,
Grandma Vivienne

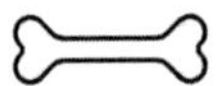

Dear Grandma Vivienne,

Pamela and Zippy are on the porch.

Pamela reads.

Zippy hunts bugs.

Catches a moth!

Tasty but powdery.

Would not be good in meatloaf.

Meatloaf is yummy without moth.

Strange man walks up to the house.

He has greasy hair.

He smells wrong.

Zippy does not like the strange man.

Zippy barks and growls.

Strange man does not stop.

Zippy leaps on the brick porch wall.

Zippy means business!

Man walks backward.

Says something to Pamela.

Zippy hears "money" and "food."

Cannot hear everything.

Too busy growling.

Pamela says, "Zippy, that's enough."

Tells man, "Wait here."

Pamela picks up Zippy.

Zippy and Pamela go into kitchen.

Pamela gets a loaf of bread and a jar of peanut butter.

Puts them in a bag.

Zippy and Pamela go back outside.

Pamela hands the bag to man.

Wait! No! Not the peanut butter!

Do we have more peanut butter?

What if we are out of peanut butter?

Zippy is worried.

Zippy forgets to growl.

Pamela takes Zippy into the house.

Pats Zippy on the head.

Says, "That was not a bad man. He was just hungry."

But Pamela thanks Zippy for protecting her from strangers.

Gives Zippy a biscuit — no peanut butter.

Calls Zippy a good guard dog.

Love,

Zippy

P.S. A kibble topping would give the meatloaf some crunch.

Cleveland Heights, Ohio
Wednesday, October 21, 1992

My dear Zippy,

My goodness! You are not just a guard dog, you are an entire Zippy Alarm System! It is always wise for children and small dogs to be wary of strangers. If only Pamela and Frank could market your skills… But I know they want to keep you – and your talents – all for themselves. And I can't say that I blame them.

There has been a further development with the cookbook. The publisher asked Pamela's mother to show him a few recipes. I suggested Winslow's Frozen Yogurt Treats, Zippy's Birthday Cake, and the new meatloaf recipe.

The publisher was so pleased, he wants to get the cookbook in print as soon as possible. He also wants as many as 50 recipes, so you and Winslow and I have to get to work in the recipe-invention-and-testing department.

Here are a few of my latest efforts:

- Cottage Cheesey Scrambled Eggs
- Kibble-Coated French Toast (I used your kibble-coating idea, but thought it would work better here than on meatloaf.)
- Chopped Chicken with Gravy
- Tea-crust Peanut Butter Sandwich Treats

You may be wondering about the tea-crust sandwiches. (The crusts are not made of tea.) When ladies make sandwiches to serve with tea, or when mothers make sandwiches for their children, they usually cut off the crusts. Often those crusts are shared with the family dog. So, I thought, why not turn the crusts into a doggy tea-time treat? I am sure you will agree that this is a good idea, especially because the filling is peanut butter.

I have already mailed these recipes and several more to Pamela. I hope she will make them for you soon so I can get your feedback. (Winslow may have to explain that word to you. I realize it sounds a bit like spitting up, which it definitely is not – unless, of course, you really hate one of the recipes.)

In the meantime, once again let me congratulate you on your security skills. Now you can add Guard Dog to your many other titles: Research Assistant, Taste Tester, Nursing Terrier… Who knows what's next for a gifted pup like you?

Love,
Grandma Vivienne

Dear Grandma Vivienne,

Pamela made the new recipes.

Kibble French toast is best, best, best!

Winslow says the scrambled eggs need Pup-Peroni pieces.

Everything is better with Pup-Peroni.

Pamela and Frank are making Chopped Chicken and Gravy tonight.

Zippy can't wait!

Love,

Zippy

Dear Grandma Vivienne,

I am writing this the morning after Zippy's letter. I thought you should know what happened last night.

Zippy and I were very excited to try the Chicken and Gravy recipe, as you can tell from her letter. I'm afraid Zippy got too excited, though.

Pamela bought the chicken, but she was out of flour for the gravy. Frank said he would go to the supermarket, and he got in his car and drove off. A lot of time passed, but Frank did not return. Pamela kept going out on the porch to look for his car.

I hesitate to tell you this, but one of the times when Pamela went on the porch, Zippy ran out the door. Maybe she thought she was running after Frank. Maybe she just didn't think. I heard Pamela yell for Zippy, but Zippy kept running. Pamela took off after her, but you know how fast that pup is.

I gleaned the rest from piecing together what I overheard Pamela say to Janet on the phone afterward. Apparently, Pamela was running around the block when she spotted Zippy at the end of the alley. Pamela quickly ran down the alley to the carport, called for Zippy, opened the car door, and Zippy ran into the car, thinking she was going for a ride.

When Pamela brought Zippy back in the house, Frank was still not here. Pamela held Zippy for a long time, then put her in her crate.

After much more time passed, the phone rang. This is what I heard Pamela say:

"No. Absolutely not. Stay overnight. Stay and think about how you ended up there. It'll do you good."

There was a long pause, then Pamela said:

"No, I am not kidding. I'll see about bail tomorrow. Sober up, Frank."

After she hung up, Pamela started to cry. That made Zippy start whimpering.

So, things are far from calm here. When you talk to Pamela, she may tell you more. I will give Zippy a talking-to about the dangers of running away, but you might want to raise the issue in your next letter. I try to set my usual stellar example, but there is only so much a wise old dog can do.

For now, I am going to sit next to Pamela's side of the bed. She didn't go into one of her frantic house-cleaning spurts. She just climbed under the covers. Like Zippy, I am no fan of the vacuum cleaner, but I think this is not a good sign.

Yours, with concern,

Winslow

CHAPTER 15

Cleveland Heights, Ohio
Friday, October 30, 1992

My dear Zippy,

Oh, boy. I see I must put on my disciplinarian's hat – something you know I hate to do. I realize that trainers say you have to discipline dogs immediately after the bad behavior, and now some time has passed.

But Zippy, this bears repeating: You did a <u>very</u> bad thing by running away. You must <u>never</u>, <u>never</u>, <u>never</u> run out the door. Not if you see a squirrel you have to chase. Not if the postman walks by. Not if you have to scare away a stranger. Not if you think you are going to find Frank. Not ever!

This is just about the worst thing you can do, and to have done it when Pamela was upset about Frank made it even worse. You are a dog of many trades, but escape artist simply <u>cannot</u> be one of them. Your most important job is to stay by Pamela's side and take care of her. Causing her more worry is unacceptable.

I regret having to scold you, but this is vital. I realize there is tension at home, but you are supposed to help relieve it, not add to it.

I have often said you can do no wrong in my eyes. Please, please, please, Zippy, be the good girl I know you are and promise <u>never</u> to run away again. I am sure you can keep this promise.

There are many dangers out there for a dog on the loose. Pamela's father, the dog judge, used to say: "A smart dog thinks and then acts. A dumb dog acts and then thinks." (Come to think of it, this is also true of people.) The point is, you are a smart dog, I love you dearly, and I want you to be around for a long time.

I spoke to Pamela about this incident, and she said she was considering crating you on Halloween. If you end up spending another Halloween in your crate, you should consider the cause of this predicament. Halloween is a fun holiday when you could be admired by all the adorable children who come to the front door. Maybe Pamela will change her mind. I hope so, and I also hope you will take this letter to heart.

Love,
Grandma Vivienne

Dear Grandma Vivienne,

Zippy did not spend Halloween in her crate.

Okay. Zippy started out in the crate.

Pamela said be quiet, Zippy, and maybe you can come out.

Zippy was quiet.

Doorbell rang. Zippy was quiet.

Doorbell rang again. Zippy was quiet.

Doorbell rang, rang, rang.

Zippy was quiet, quiet, quiet.

Not easy.

Zippy thought Pamela forgot.

Then Pamela took Zippy out of the crate!

Pamela put devil's horns on Zippy.

Zippy did not like the devil's horns, but better than being in the crate.

Pamela held Zippy under her arm.

Zippy greeted children.

Lots of fun.

One boy dressed in devil costume.

He said Zippy should be his devil dog.

Pamela would not let Zippy go.

Pamela held Zippy tight.

Pamela loves Zippy.

Zippy loves Pamela.

Zippy will not run away again.

Love,

Zippy

P.S. Pamela made Chopped Chicken and Gravy!

Yummy!

Frank did not help.

Frank is not here.

Cleveland Heights, Ohio
Friday, November 20, 1992

My dear Zippy,

Winslow has probably explained that Frank is in the hospital again. This is a different hospital. A judge – yes, like the judges on "Law & Order" – sent him to this hospital. I don't know when he will be back.

Just as it was a bad thing when you nearly disappeared, it is a bad thing when Frank disappears. The last time was especially scary.

But I also have good news: Pamela's mother is coming to Baltimore to spend Thanksgiving with you and Winslow and Pamela. She will cook the turkey herself, which means she will be in charge of the turkey liver and will probably give it to Winslow. (She was quite upset by your recent attempted escape and may feel you need to earn the special privilege of the turkey liver.) Being the gentleman he is, however, Winslow might be willing to share it with you, and who knows? Maybe you'll even score some giblets.

Pamela's mother can try out more recipes for the cookbook during her visit, and you and Winslow can perform your role as taste testers.

She will be there on Tuesday afternoon. Pamela is taking her to the theater. They will be seeing a show called "Cats" (but maybe I shouldn't mention that…).

Anyway, this is only a few days away. So prepare to be on your best behavior and some yummy new meals and treats will be your reward.

Love,
Grandma Vivienne

P.S. I am not sure if you have been following the news, but we will soon have a new president – a Democrat named Bill Clinton. He and his running mate won even though, right before the election, President Bush said, "My dog Millie knows more about foreign affairs than these two bozos." I am well aware of your opinion of Millie, and I assure you, our new leader is far more knowledgeable – and diplomatic – than she is.

I do not know if Bill Clinton and his family have a dog, but I will try to find out.

Dear Grandma Vivienne,

Is Pamela's mother better now?

Zippy is an excellent Nursing Terrier.

Zippy visited her in the hospital.

Zippy visited other patients.

Zippy would like to give every patient a tennis ball.

Tennis balls are happy medicine.

Pamela's mother should be all better.

Zippy brought her lots of tennis balls.

Love,

Zippy, RNT (Registered Nursing Terrier)

Cleveland Heights, Ohio
Wednesday, December 16, 1992

My dear Zippy,

Yes, indeed, you are an excellent Nursing Terrier. And Pamela's mother truly appreciated the get-well cards you and Winslow sent her. I cannot imagine how Zippy found a card with a picture of a dog that looked so much like her!

The doctor in Cleveland has started Pamela's mother on radiation treatments. (These are not the same as the radio Pamela turns on for you when she goes out, although both, I suppose, can have a healing effect.)

Pamela's mother certainly never expected to celebrate Thanksgiving in the hospital, much less undergo lung surgery. But one thing we can all be thankful for is that Baltimore has one of the best hospitals in the world, and the doctors there caught her illness early.

I think her recovery began as soon as Pamela snuck you into her hospital room. I still don't know how she managed it, but I suspect it may have been inspired by "Zippy Goes to Bermuda."

True, breaking away from Pamela and running loose was not a smart thing to do. I have reproached you severely about this behavior in the past. But when Pamela told me how the patients — well, most of the patients — smiled and laughed as you dashed in and out of their rooms, I have to give you some slack.

I realize you must have been disappointed when Pamela's mother did not respond with gusto to all of the tennis balls you dropped at her feet after she got back to your house. Who knew you had so many tennis balls tucked away?

And though your brand of "on-the-patient" care – as Frank puts it – had to be restrained due to her incision, your companionship alone seems to have had a positive effect on Pamela's mother's spirits.

Her doctor in Cleveland said Pamela's mother could return to the classroom if she felt up to it, and with less than a week left before Christmas vacation, we just managed to finish helping the art students make their holiday-themed gifts. Most made ornaments again this year, but a few made Christmas stockings, and one or two of these were for their pets.

I plan to devote much of my vacation to working with Pamela's mother on the cookbook. I think we should create some new holiday-themed dog biscuits. We will send you and Winslow the results.

Speaking of holidays, Hanukkah begins Saturday, and along with your other presents, one of your gifts will be Frank's return home. He will definitely be happy to see you, but, again, I am not sure that tormenting – did I write that? I meant "greeting" – him with piles of tennis balls will be the best welcome. I am sure you can come up with a greeting that is equally heartfelt, but perhaps less overwhelming.

Love,
Grandma Vivienne

P.S. Please share this with Winslow: According to news reports, President Clinton and his family do not have a dog. They will be moving into the White House with a cat named "Socks." Socks is black with white paws, a white chest, and a white blaze on his face. He is, in fact, marked like a Boston Terrier.

There has never been an actual Boston Terrier in the White House, even though Bostons are among the few all-American breeds. Perhaps you and Winslow could write a letter to the National Boston Terrier Club encouraging them to give the Clintons a Boston. Just think of all the cute photo ops with these two black-and-white pets!

CHAPTER 16

National Boston Terrier Club
P.O. Box 55513
Boston, MA 02205

Dear National Boston Terrier Club,

It has come to our attention that President-Elect William Jefferson Clinton and his family will be moving into the White House without a presidential dog.

We would like to suggest that the club donate a puppy to the Clintons. We have it on good authority that there has never been a Boston in the White House, and it would be excellent publicity for this all-American breed. We are aware that the Clintons own a cat, and we are certain that the Boston puppy and the cat would get along so well, they would be a model of diplomatic relations.

We trust you will give our suggestion serious consideration, and we look forward to hearing from you. This is a matter of national importance.

Sincerely,

Winslow (a proud Boston Terrier)
&
Zippy (a friend of Boston Terriers everywhere)

cc: President-Elect William Jefferson Clinton

Cleveland Heights, Ohio
Sunday, December 27, 1992

My dear Zippy,

What a beautiful letter you and Winslow wrote to the National Boston Terrier Club! I suspect Winslow did most of the writing, but Zippy, I am sure you provided enthusiastic support. The copy that you sent me was one of my favorite Hanukkah presents. Pamela told me how quickly you devoured the tin of dreidel- and Star of David-shaped Hanukkah biscuits I made for you, so I know that gift was well-received!

I am sure you are enjoying having Frank back home. Please do not feel left out when he and Winslow go out without you in the mornings. This is therapeutic for Frank, and Winslow is a steadying presence.

Pamela's mother is now getting respiratory

therapy. I drive her to a rehabilitation center that does all types of therapy, and though she is what is called an "out patient," there are plenty of "in patients." These patients stay there for extended periods, until they are capable of functioning at home.

This got me thinking that Pamela might call some rehab centers in Baltimore to see if they would be interested in having a Therapy Dog – you! – visit their patients. Who knows? Some might even welcome your on-the-patient care. At the very least, you would be a ray of sunshine during this cold, gray winter.

Give it some thought. You've already shown you have the spirit of a Therapy Dog. Also let me know what you hear from the National Boston Terrier Club about a presidential puppy.

Love & best wishes for a happy, healthy New Year,
Grandma Vivienne

Dear Grandma Vivienne,

Zippy and Winslow saw President Clinton sworn in.

Should presidents swear?

Zippy watched for a long time.

Saw the President dancing.

Saw the President's wife.

Saw the President's daughter.

Did not see a Boston Terrier puppy.

Did not even see Socks the cat.

Zippy is very disappointed in President Clinton.

Zippy is giving up on politics.

Zippy is going into medicine.

Love,

Zippy, RNT, STT (Spirited Therapy Terrier)

P.S. No letter from the National Boston Terrier Club.

Nobody writes to Zippy except Grandma Vivienne!

Cleveland Heights, Ohio
Wednesday, January 27, 1993

My dear Zippy,

I understand your disappointment with President Clinton, but I think your hurt feelings may be misdirected.

After I read your wonderful letter to the National Boston Club, I followed up with a letter of my own. I am afraid I have not heard back, either.

Do not give up on politics and President Clinton. This is just the start of his presidency, and I am sure he has many equally important matters to attend to.

In the meantime, I am working on a Valentine surprise for you and Winslow. Keep watch for a package in the next week or so (I know the comings and goings of the mailman are a crucial part of your day).

Love,
Grandma Vivienne

P.S. I have spoken to Pamela. She is going to call Janet to find out where you can get Therapy Dog training.

Dear Grandma Vivienne,

Valentine scarves are pretty.

Valentine scarves are soft.

Hearts on scarves are pretty.

Pamela put a scarf on Winslow.

Zippy pulled the scarf off Winslow.

Ran around the house with it.

Chewed Winslow's scarf.

Does not taste good.

Pamela put a scarf on Zippy.

Zippy shook the scarf off.

Not as good as pink Valentine biscuits.

Zippy ate every biscuit.

Please send more biscuits.

Do not send more scarves.

Love,

Zippy

P.S. Zippy has started Therapy Dog School. Training does not require Zippy to wear scarf.

Dear Grandma Vivienne,

I am not usually a fan of canine couture — except, of course, functional attire, like sweaters, which keep a fellow warm. However, the red Valentine scarf you made for me was very dapper — before Zippy got to it. (I thought that animal had learned her lesson after chewing up the sweater you knitted for me a couple years back.)

Pamela has given me Zippy's Valentine scarf as a

replacement, and she ties it in a way that looks as if I'm wearing a bow tie. Pink isn't really my color, but it's still a rather snappy look — though perhaps "snappy" isn't the best word considering what Zippy's mandibles did to my scarf (and to that sweater, but I pride myself on letting bygones be bygones...).

How is Pamela's mother feeling? I don't think Zippy understood how serious a health scare she had. Zippy was just glad to have extra time at home with Pamela's mother after the doctors decided she should have surgery in Baltimore, where Pamela could take care of her. And I, of course, also was glad for the extra time together.

I don't know if I should bring this up, but after her mother went back to Cleveland, Pamela was truly exhausted. She spent a lot of time asleep on the sofa or in bed, with Zippy snuggled up next to her. Since her return to work, she's been staying at the office late into the night.

Frank has only been of limited help, cooking a meal here and there or taking Zippy and me for a brief perambulation. This is always a slow time in the landscaping trade, but I haven't seen him look at a single blueprint. Nor has he been taking me on walks to his meetings at the church lately. The next time he does, I promise to wear my Valentine's "bow tie."

Also, as you can tell from Zippy's letter, I did not get a single nibble of the Valentine biscuits. If it's not too much trouble, I would be most grateful if you could send a few more, marked to my attention, and purely for taste-testing purposes, of course.

These biscuits, and the Hanukkah ones before them, have given me an idea. Perhaps the recipes in the cookbook could focus on holiday victuals. All I ask is a mention in the acknowledgements — and some seasonal samples.

Gratefully yours,

Winslow, The Dapper Dog

Cleveland Heights, Ohio
Friday, March 5, 1993

My dear Zippy,

I am glad the Valentine biscuits were a hit, but I understand that Winslow did not get his fair share - or any at all, for that matter. Enthusiasm is a good thing, Zippy, but you must learn restraint.

For example, while you had a great deal of fun with Winslow's scarf, that was not its intended purpose. The weather gets cold in Baltimore, and I thought some warmth around each of your necks might be welcome, like a hug from Grandma. Now you will have to make do without your Valentine hug.

Pamela's mother's art students made Valentines for each other, and the entire class presented her with a giant heart, which they all signed. Very sweet.

I have big news! Please tell Winslow that the cookbook publisher loves the idea of a cookbook of holiday recipes for dogs and wants to go to press as soon as possible!

Please also tell him that Pamela's mother is feeling much stronger. I am concerned that she is doing too much too soon, so every chance I get, I try to do her share of the work along with mine.

Right now, we are busily concocting new recipes. The latest is a Hanukkah stew with beef, peas, and carrots. We have also come up with a New Year's giblet paté that I know you will love.

Unfortunately, the publisher did not go for my idea of using illustrations by some of the after-school art students. Instead, he wants Pamela's mother to illustrate the book. She, in turn, wants me to do it. I guess that makes me a "ghost illustrator" as well as "ghost writer." Who knows? With the cookbook and "Zippy Goes to Bermuda," I could have a new career as an illustrator!

I have set up the drafting table and taped photos of you and Winslow around the edges. I am working on drawings of you both. I have enclosed sketches in two different styles. Let me know which you prefer.

Winslow told me how you stuck close by Pamela after her mother flew back to Cleveland. Once again, you have proved to have the true instincts of an outstanding Therapy Dog. I am so glad you are taking classes! This is good for Pamela as well as for you.

Please try not to be frustrated, however, by the long hours she is putting in at the newspaper. As you will learn, a Therapy Dog adjusts his – or her – behavior to a person's needs. For now, Pamela needs to stay later because she missed so much work. Just continue to be your cheerful self whenever she walks in the door, and treats and head pats are sure to come your way.

Got to go. Lot of work ahead!

Love,
Grandma Vivienne

Hearty Hanukkah Stew

- 16 oz. stewing beef, cut into cubes
- 2 14.5-oz. cans of beef stock
- 1 teaspoon flour
- 1 12-oz. bag of frozen peas
- 4 carrots, skinned & chopped
- 2 medium potatoes, skinned & cut into cubes
- 2 oz. canola or vegetable oil

Brown meat in oil in stockpot. Add beef stock. After stock boils, lower temperature to simmer for 30 minutes, covered. Add potatoes and carrots. Whisk teaspoon of flour in a little cold water, then stir into stew. Simmer for another 30 minutes. Add peas and simmer for 15 more minutes, uncovered.

Dear Grandma Vivienne,

Snow snow snow snow snow!!!

Snow everywhere!!!

Where is Zippy's scarf?

Pamela opened the back door to let Zippy out.

Zippy went down one step, two steps, three steps.

Where are the other steps?

Whoops!!!!!

Zippy is buried in snow.

Can't get out! Can't get out! Can't get out!

Help Zippy!

Pamela dug Zippy out.

Pamela called for Frank:

"Come quick with the camera."

Pamela and Frank laughed.

Not funny!

Zippy is cold.

Zippy is wet.

Zippy is not going out in the snow again.

Ever.

Ask Pamela to take Zippy to Bermuda.

More research.

No snow.

Love,

Zippy

P.S. Send warm weather.

P.P.S. Zippy loves her drawing.

Today's drawing of Zippy would be blank.

White dog in white snow.

P.P.P.S. Send warm weather NOW!

Cleveland Heights, Ohio
Wednesday, March 24, 1993

My dear Zippy,

My goodness! What an ordeal! The blizzard on the East Coast made national news. I wish I could send you warm weather, but it is very cold here, too. You will have to be patient, although I realize this does not come easily to you.

The cookbook publisher is not patient, either. The text and illustrations are due in a few weeks, and Pamela's mother has me working day and night. The publisher has all kinds of plans for marketing the book in pet stores as well as bookstores. He even said something about "personal appearances."

He did not say anything about "canine appearances," but I would certainly think that you and Winslow should come along, at least for some of the appearances. Wouldn't that be fun?

No time to write more now. Back to the drafting table.

Love,
Grandma Vivienne

P.S. In case it makes you feel any warmer, Spring officially began three days ago.
P.P.S. Pamela cannot take you to Bermuda. Remember? That was why she came up with the idea for the children's book. Maybe I should encourage her to get back to that…

CHAPTER 17

Little Zippy's turning three,
Still as cute as she can be!
And to make the day complete:
Here's a homemade birthday treat.
From now on, it bears your name.
Maybe it will bring you fame!
Love,
Grandma Vivienne

Enclosed note: Believe it or not, Zippy, Pamela's mother and I — which means, mostly me — have finished all of the cookbook text and illustrations. We are now focusing on naming the recipes. The birthday cake is, of course, still named for you. And in honor of this year's birthday, and remembering your fondness for my holiday biscuits, they are now called: "Zippy's Favorite Everyday's-A-Holiday Treat."

I can just imagine public appearances with you seated beside a bowl of your "Everyday's-A-Holiday Treats," available to any dog whose owner purchases a cookbook.

But I am getting ahead of myself. We turn in everything at the end of the week, and we will see what happens from there.

Finally, Zippy, please give at least one of your birthday treats to Winslow.

Happy Birthday!

Dear Grandma Vivienne,

Zippy will be famous!

Zippy will guard her Everyday's-A-Holiday Treats!

Zippy will demonstrate how delicious they are!

When do we start?

Pamela took Zippy to visit rehab patients.

Big success!

Lots of pats on the head.

Lots of smiles.

No on-the-patient care.

Love,

Zippy

P.S. Zippy thinks you should name a recipe for Grandma Vivienne.

Something sweet.

P.P.S. Zippy also thinks you should name a recipe for Pamela.

Something guaranteed to make her smile.

Maybe cookies that look like tennis balls.

P.P.P.S. Zippy even thinks you should name a recipe for Winslow.

Something Zippy doesn't like.

Something with broccoli.

Cleveland Heights, Ohio
Wednesday, April 28, 1993

My dear Zippy,

Big news: The publisher likes the cookbook! The editor is doing some fine tuning, but the book could be published as soon as July or August! And here's more exciting news: The publisher wants Pamela's mother to do a few pre-publication appearances, probably in late May or early June.

One of these appearances is at a big dog show in Pittsburgh. I am trying to convince Pamela's mother that you and Pamela and Winslow and Frank should come. There will be a booth dedicated to the book with a large poster of the cover and sample treats made from the recipes, just as I imagined.

Having you and Winslow there would be a great asset. And Zippy, this would be a real coup for you. Dog shows, as I believe I have explained, are strictly for purebred dogs. By taking your rightful place in the booth, you will be a proud representative of all mixed-breed dogs everywhere.

So, the dog show will not only be fun for you, it will be a political act! I will ask Pamela to check her schedule.

Love,
Grandma Vivienne

Dear Grandma Vivienne,

The cookbook is here!

A drawing of Zippy and Winslow is on the cover!

More drawings of Zippy and Winslow are inside!

Why is the cover so thin?

This is a serious book.

Serious books must have hard covers.

Zippy and Winslow are coming to Pittsburgh.

Zippy will be a star!

Love,

Zippy

Dear Grandma Vivienne,

The cookbook is a triumph! A work of art! A gastronomic chef d'oeuvre (pun on "chef" intended)! And the title, "Food for the Dogs: Easy Holiday Recipes You Can Make for Your Dog," is nearly perfect. Astute readers will surely recognize that "food for the dogs" is witty wordplay for "food for the gods." I do think you might have chosen a slightly more highbrow subtitle, however — something on the order of "A Culinary Compendium for Canine Celebrations."

But I quibble. I've always been a sucker for alliterative titles. Yet I realize your publisher may be aiming for a broader audience than just those of us who savor the occasional bon mot.

Pamela showed us the book, page by page, on the sofa. Zippy

was seated on her left, and I was on her right. Yes, I confess, I sat on the sofa. It was a special occasion. And I was glad to be securely ensconced next to Pamela because the dedication left me so moved, I started to shake: "To Winslow and Zippy, without whom this book would not have happened, and especially to Pamela and her dad."

I cannot begin to express how honored I am. Although I pride myself on being a bibliophilic Boston, I never imagined seeing my name in a book. Nor is it lost on me that you put my name first.

It is also not lost on me that you left out Frank's name. I know he had very little to do with this book. So perhaps that was your reason.

Zippy is in a total tizzy about the flimsy cover. I tried to explain that this volume is merely a proof, but she got that all mixed up with "proof of innocence" and "proof of guilt" from "Law & Order." I didn't even attempt to call it a "galley." Instead, I tried "first draft," but she thought that had something to do with wind and breezes and got worried that the book would blow away. Maybe you can come up with an explanation she'll understand.

Yours,

Winslow, Esteemed Book Critic

Cleveland Heights, Ohio
Wednesday, May 26, 1993

My dear Zippy,

Let me set your mind at ease about the cookbook's cover. The copy I sent you is not the finished version. It is only a sample, an example of what the finished book will look like. The final version will definitely have a hard cover, and the drawing on the cover will be in color, not black and white. So there is no need to fret. You will not be disappointed.

I am afraid, however, that I do have one bit of disappointing news. The appearance at the Pittsburgh dog show has been cancelled. Pamela's mother developed another bad cough, and her doctor is concerned. He doesn't want her to weaken her heart as well as her lungs, and he insisted she get more rest. When Pamela heard this, she wanted to come visit, but her mother told her she has already taken too much time off.

Zippy, I am sure there will be other appearances, including book signings, when the final version of the cookbook is in print. You will be able to stand next to – or sit on top of! – a stack of hard-cover books. You and Winslow can be the Official Spokesdogs for "Food for the Dogs." ("Spokesdog," however, does not mean unlimited barking.)

Pamela's mother and I were thinking that you both might sign some copies with paw prints. Let me know if that appeals to you.

Love,

Grandma Vivienne

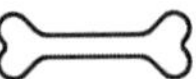

Dear Grandma Vivienne,

No Pittsburgh business trip for Zippy and Winslow.

How is Pamela's mother?

Frank went to New York on an overnight business trip.

He drove to New York.

He did not take Zippy or Winslow.

Winslow says that was a big mistake.

Winslow calls himself Frank's sponsor.

He says a sponsor should always be nearby.

Zippy does not know what "sponsor" means.

Frank did not come home for days and days and days and...

Then Frank came home without the car.

Winslow said he took a bus.

Where is the car?

Zippy loves to ride in the car.

Pamela says Frank is not getting a new car.

She says Frank is not driving again for a long time.

Frank is sleeping at his office.

Zippy has an idea about the cookbook.

Zippy will write a message for everyone who buys a book.

The message will say:

"Thank you for buying this wonderful cookbook.

You will love the wonderful recipes in this wonderful book.

Signed,

Zippy and Winslow."

Paw print. Paw print.

Zippy will work on a way to type messages on small pieces of paper.

Winslow can help.

That will cheer Winslow up.

Pamela says she and Winslow are in the doldrums.

What kind of drums are doldrums?

Are doldrums loud?

It is very quiet around here.

Love,

Zippy

Cleveland Heights, Ohio
Wednesday, June 16, 1993

My dear Zippy,

Pamela's mother is feeling better each day. She and I love the idea of including your message in each book purchased at one of the personal appearances. And, we have come up with a way to make it work, without slips of paper. We are going to have a rubber stamp made with your message. We will stamp the message in each book purchased at an appearance that you attend, and then you and Winslow can add your paw prints.

Pamela's mother is scheduled to be a guest on a Cleveland TV show in two weeks. I have already started coaching her. I will let you know how it goes.

As to Frank no longer having a car, this is troubling for more reasons than not being able to take you for rides. He also no longer has a driver's license. Without going into what happened, I will say that sometimes a near catastrophe, like the one Frank just had, can be the start of a cure. I hope so, for his sake and Pamela's.

Love,
Grandma Vivienne

P.S. Doldrums are not drums. They are not loud. They are low spirits and often very quiet.

Dear Grandma Vivienne,

Zippy did not know Frank had a near catastrophe.

That explains it.

In Zippy's experience, cats are nothing but trouble.

They tease Zippy.

They make Zippy chase them,

then they run up trees or onto fences

where Zippy can't catch them.

Not nice.

Not fun.

How was the TV show?

Pamela and Frank have two TVs.

Pamela's mother was not on either one.

Why not?

Did Pamela's mother mention Zippy and Winslow on TV?

She must have.

Without Zippy and Winslow, "this book would not have happened."

Frank still is not sleeping here.

He comes home when Pamela is at the office.

He works in the garden.

He picks flowers for Pamela.

Zippy helps.

Pansies taste good.

Love,

Zippy

Cleveland Heights, Ohio
Wednesday, July 14, 1993

My dear Zippy,

By now you should have received the copy I sent you of the finished book, with a hard cover.

You may have noticed that in addition to naming many recipes for you and Winslow, I have taken your suggestion and named a few for me, such as Vivienne's Granola Biscuits and Vivienne's Kibble Gravy. I figured if Pamela's mother wouldn't put my name on the cover, or in the dedication or acknowledgments, why shouldn't I grab some credit inside?

I am sorry you were unable to see the TV

interview. It was only broadcast in Cleveland. If there is ever a TV interview in Baltimore, maybe you and Winslow could appear on TV, too!

Next week Pamela's mother will be at a cookbook convention in Boston. She will be interested to see if there are any other books of recipes for dogs. I wish you and Winslow and Pamela could be there, but Pamela will be covering a theater festival in Chicago for the newspaper.

Wait! I have an idea. Pamela could put you on an airplane to Boston, and her mother could pick you up and take you to the convention! (Maybe the publisher would pay for it.) Wouldn't that be fun?! I will ask Pamela.

Love,
Grandma Vivienne

Dear Grandma Vivienne,

Zippy is going to fly an airplane.

Just like Snoopy.

Zippy needs a helmet and white scarf and goggles.

Why has Pamela brought the crate upstairs?

Love,

Zippy

Dear Grandma Vivienne,

As you can see, the silly pup thinks she will be piloting the airplane, not merely riding in it. When she finds herself in her crate in cargo, I suspect she may be less cheerful. But who knows? Zippy is always up for an adventure. She might actually enjoy being in the airborne equivalent of steerage.

I wanted to bring up an idea: When Pamela's mother is checking out competing books of dog recipes at the convention, maybe she could also check out cookbooks for children. My thinking is that if she could connect Pamela with a children's book publisher, that might reawaken her interest in "Zippy Goes to Bermuda." Working on that silly book about our silly pup could be just the diversion Pamela needs now.

Without intending to upset you, I mention this because Pamela would benefit considerably from what theater folk call "comic relief." She has been fretting herself into a frenzy. Along with her concerns about Frank, she has become extremely worried about her mother's health. Lately, she has been bringing home medical texts. She reads these in bed, and I can tell they are interfering with her sleep. When she tosses and turns, Zippy leaps onto the bed and curls up next to her. This does appear to have a soporific effect, at least on Zippy.

Well, while Pamela's mother and Zippy are galavanting around Boston, and Pamela is reviewing a dozen plays in three days in Chicago, Frank will be staying at the house, taking care of me. This will be the first time he has been in residence since the car accident, and I have a feeling I will be taking care of him. Perhaps if I steer him toward the neighborhood church on our morning walk, I can get him to stop in at some meetings. As his unofficial sponsor, I will do my best.

I look forward to hearing all about the convention. Wish I could be there with Zippy, but I have important work to do here. I miss Frank the way he used to be — smart, funny, creative. I know Pamela does, too. She and I truly believe he can get better, but I'm not sure he believes it.

Sincerely,

Winslow, the Diligent

Cleveland Heights, Ohio
Wednesday, July 28, 1993

My dear Zippy,

I am relieved that you are back home safely. Pamela's mother is convinced that your mere presence sold some books – even when you went dashing around the convention hall grabbing samples from almost every booth… Pamela's mother was <u>very</u> grateful to the security guard who managed to snatch you up. She was afraid you were headed out the door and into Boston traffic.

While not condoning your antics, she acknowledged that the chaos you created did bring extra attention to her booth. But Zippy, this tendency of yours to take off has got to stop. Now!

Winslow was smart to suggest checking out the children's cookbook publishers. Riley Publishing has one of the largest and most diverse catalogues of children's literature, and Pamela's mother believes that meeting you, the title character of "Zippy Goes to Bermuda," sealed the deal, especially because the Riley representative was conveniently out of the exhibition hall when you embarked on your high-speed race.

So, although Pamela's mother may think twice before taking you to any future conventions, she clearly appreciated your help at this one. Maybe there will be some smaller appearances coming up.

Love,
Grandma Vivienne

Dear Grandma Vivienne,

The convention was fun!

The airplane was not fun.

NOISE NOISE NOISE NOISE NOISE NOISE!!!

Zippy never heard so much noise.

Zippy never made so much noise.

In her life.

Zippy barked and barked and barked.

Great big gray Poodle barked and barked and barked.

Zippy got a better idea at the convention.

Zippy would run home.

No airplane.

Zippy started to run.

The food samples were too tempting.

Zippy almost forgot to run out the door.

Got caught.

The samples were yummy.

Beef jerky was very very very yummy.

Salad was not yummy.

Slimey stuff on top.

Pizza bagels were yummy.

Sushi was more slimey.

Beef jerky was the best.

Zippy will do more public appearances.

Zippy promises to behave.

The airplane ride home was more NOISE.

Zippy had to bark and bark and bark all over again.

No giant gray Poodles. No other dogs.

Zippy had to bark by herself.

Zippy will not fly anymore —

unless Zippy can ride in the cockpit like Snoopy.

Where is Zippy's next public appearance?

Love,

Zippy

CHAPTER 18

Cleveland Heights, Ohio
Friday, August 20, 1993

My dear Zippy,

I am delighted to report that the next cookbook signing will be at a dog show in Wilmington, Delaware, over the Labor Day weekend. Wilmington is not a long drive from Baltimore, so Pamela can easily bring you and Winslow. No airplanes. You can be the co-pilot of Pamela's car.

Pamela is planning to meet her mother there the second day of the show, when her mother will give a short cooking demonstration. Her mother's doctor does not want her to make this trip, but she insists. And this is one of the rare times when I agree with her. Indeed, the trip could have a positive effect on her health. It is an easy flight, and she will be doing something she enjoys. So Wilmington, here she comes.

She probably will keep you on a leash at this event. Quite honestly, Pamela's mother was terrified that she would never see you again when you started running in Boston.

What matters most is that you are safe and that you will have another chance to prove what a well-behaved asset you can be in promoting the cookbook.

Love,
Grandma Vivienne

Dear Grandma Vivienne,

Why no dog show?

Why no cooking demonstration?

Pamela, Winslow and Co-Pilot Zippy headed to Wilmington.

Pamela stopped at a gas station.

"Relax, guys. Time for coffee."

Pamela rolled down the window enough for Zippy's nose.

Not enough to leap out and run after her.

Zippy and Winslow stared out the window and waited.

A long time.

Pamela got in the car.

Put her head in her hands.

Cried.

A lot.

Pamela pounded her fist on the steering wheel.

Zippy and Winslow jumped.

Zippy yelped.

Pamela reached over and petted Zippy.

“It’s okay, guys.

It’s okay.”

Pamela cried some more.

Zippy whimpered to keep her company.

Pamela whispered, “It’s not okay. It’s not okay.

Let’s go home now.”

Pamela started the car.

No talking. No radio.

Zippy loves car rides.

This ride not fun.

Frank came out on the porch.

“Pamela, thank God you called. I couldn’t reach you.”

Frank hugged Pamela.

Pamela said, "I have to go back now."

Back to the dog show?

Pamela carried Zippy inside.

Winslow followed.

Zippy licked Pamela's face.

Salty.

Pamela put Zippy on the sofa.

Pamela drove away.

Did Pamela and her mother go to the dog show without Zippy and Winslow?

Why?

Please explain.

Love,

Zippy

Dear Grandma Vivienne,

Frank is going to Cleveland.

Pamela is in Cleveland.

Zippy and Winslow are not going.

Why not?

Frank got a new suit.

Frank calls it his sincere black suit.

He put the suit in a suitcase.

Zippy jumped in the suitcase.

Zippy will go to Cleveland just like Zippy went to Bermuda!

Frank says, "No, Zippy."

Zippy does not understand.

Everyone is leaving.

Zippy is going to sleep in Winslow's dog bed with Winslow.

Love,

Zippy

Dear Grandma Vivienne,

Janet is coming to stay with Zippy and Winslow.

Why?

Winslow does not explain.

Winslow wanders around the house.

Winslow hangs his head.

Zippy thinks Winslow is back in the doldrums.

Winslow jumped on the bed and laid down on Pamela's pillow.

Pamela will be upset with Winslow.

Zippy jumped on the pillow next to Winslow.

Why is Pamela in Cleveland?

Zippy needs a letter from Grandma Vivienne.

Is Grandma Vivienne on a cruise with Pamela's mother?

Please write and explain.

Love,

Zippy

Dear Grandma Vivienne,

Where are your letters?

Where are your postcards?

Where are you?

Where?

Winslow says nothing.

Zippy looks all over.

Pulls the mail out of the mail slot.

Chews some envelopes.

Zippy can't find a letter from Grandma Vivienne.

Please write.

Love,

Zippy

Dear Grandma Vivienne,

Pamela is back from Cleveland.

Pamela holds Zippy and cries.

Zippy's fur gets wet.

Pamela rests her head against wet Zippy.

Winslow lies at Pamela's feet.

Zippy found a card from Janet.

"Deepest condolences on the loss of your mother."

What are condolences?

Is Pamela's mother lost?

Does she need a map?

Is Grandma Vivienne looking for Pamela's mother?

Frank has not been home in days.

Is Frank looking for Pamela's mother?

Zippy misses letters from Grandma Vivienne.

Zippy misses Grandma Vivienne.

Please write.

Love,

Zippy

Dear Grandma Vivienne,

Pamela sits in the wing chair.

Zippy curls up on her lap.

Winslow leans against Pamela's legs.

Pamela pets Winslow and Zippy.

"You are such good dogs."

More tears.

Zippy jumps off Pamela's lap and gets a tennis ball.

Drops the tennis ball at her feet.

Gets more tennis balls.

Tennis balls make everyone happy.

Pamela says, "Not now, Zippy."

Pamela picks Zippy up.

Pamela hugs Zippy for a long time.

"Zippy is a good Therapy Dog.

We are going to finish therapy training.

That'll be fun.

Maybe we'll finish Zippy Goes to Bermuda.

Maybe we'll write a different book.

But no more letters."

Why not?

Zippy likes to write letters.

Pamela has stopped crying.

Zippy's fur is still wet.

Zippy doesn't mind being a wet dog.

PLEASE write.

Please.

Love,

Zippy

Dear Grandma Vivienne,

Pamela and Zippy and Winslow are going on the book tour!

Pamela's mother is not going.

Winslow says Pamela's mother and Grandma Vivienne are with the Dog Judge.

Winslow says they are not coming back.

Zippy has never met the Dog Judge.

Every time somebody mentions him, they say he is late.

Maybe that's why we haven't met.

Zippy is glad Grandma Vivienne is not alone.

Zippy thinks Grandma Vivienne would not want us to be sad all the time.

Pamela did not cry yesterday.

Not once.

Winslow says continuing the tour will help the cookbook.

The tour will help Pamela.

Winslow and Zippy will help Pamela.

Pamela packs a suitcase.

Zippy hides tennis balls in the suitcase.

Zippy is writing because Grandma Vivienne needs to know Zippy is okay.

And Winslow is okay.

And Pamela will be okay.

Winslow says Frank will also be okay.

He is staying with a friend from the meetings in the church basement.

Zippy wants to make sure Grandma Vivienne receives this letter.

Please, Grandma Vivienne, if there is a post office anywhere near you,

please,

just one more time,

please write.

Love,

Zippy

For Additional Reading, Viewing, and Listening

Archy and Mehitabel, Don Marquis

Archy and Mehitabel / Carnival of the Animals, CD, performed by Carol Channing, Eddie Bracken, and David Wayne

The Griffin & Sabine Trilogy, Nick Bantock

The Guernsey Literary and Potato Peel Pie Society, Mary Ann Shaffer and Annie Barrows

Ella Minnow Pea, Mark Dunn

Elisabeth Mann Borgese's Talking Dog https://www.youtube.com/watch?v=ZGKmRA0pWhs

You Had Me at Woof: How Dogs Taught Me the Secrets of Happiness, Julie Klam

Huck: The Remarkable True Story of How One Lost Puppy Taught a Family — and a Whole Town — About Hope and Happy Endings, Janet Elder

E.B. White on Dogs, edited by Martha White

The Last Will and Testament of an Extremely Distinguished Dog, Eugene O'Neill

Investigations of a Dog, Franz Kafka

Flush, Virginia Woolf

Marley & Me, John Grogan

A Dog's Journey and *A Dog's Purpose*, W. Bruce Cameron

Rin Tin Tin: The Life and the Legend, Susan Orleans

Sylvia, A.R. Gurney

Sandy: The Autobiography of a Star, as told to William Berloni and Allison Thomas

The Boston Terrier, E. J. Rousuck

Best in Show, movie, directed by Christopher Guest

After Great Pain: A New Life Emerges, Diane Cole

About Alice, Calvin Trillin

Unforgettable: A Son, A Mother, and The Lessons of a Lifetime, Scott Simon

Notes on Grief, Chimamanda Ngozi Adichie

A Dog Is Listening: The Way Some of Our Closest Friends View Us, Roger A. Caras

Inside of a Dog: What Dogs See, Smell, and Know, Alexandra Horowitz

Walkies: Dog Training & Care the Woodhouse Way, Barbara Woodhouse

Book Club Discussion Questions for *Please Write*, by J. Wynn Rousuck

1. How did the author's choice to write an epistolary novel affect your reading experience?

2. What do the different writing styles of Winslow, Zippy, and Vivienne tell you about their personalities?

3. What does Vivienne's perspective bring to the narrative? Discuss her role in relation to Pamela, Winslow, and Zippy.

4. Why do you think Pamela is so opposed to Zippy at the beginning? Why does she change her mind?

5. Why is Winslow opposed to Zippy at first? What changes his mind?

6. Which character did you connect with the most and why?

7. The power of imagination is one of the novel's central themes. Where in the book is this power most evident?

8. Rousuck has said one of her goals for the book is to help readers who are struggling with hardship and loss. How does the story touch on these themes and offer solace?

9. Discuss how humor is used in the book to balance darker themes. What impact did this combination have on your overall appreciation of the novel?

10. How would you describe the role of dogs in the novel, especially in terms of companionship and healing? Can you relate to this in your own life?

11. How does the early 1990s setting shape the narrative? How would the story differ if it were set in the present day?

12. Do you find *Please Write* more character-driven or plot-driven? How did this affect your enjoyment of the novel?

13. In what ways do you think Rousuck's background as a theater critic might have influenced her writing in *Please Write*? Can you imagine *Please Write* as a play? A movie?

14. Now that you've read the book, discuss the significance of the title, *Please Write*.

15. Rousuck hopes the novel might inspire readers to write a letter or two. After reading the book, are you inclined to do so? Why or why not?

16. If there were a sequel to *Please Write*, what do you think it would be about?

Acknowledgments

More than a dozen years into my tenure as the theater critic of *The Baltimore Sun*, I attended a daylong workshop for journalists taught by playwright Paula Vogel. The Pulitzer Prize winner believes "everybody's an artist, and everybody can write plays" — even theater critics. During the lunch break, she assigned us to write one of three types of short plays: A play about a dog; a monolog; or a play that's impossible to stage. Unable to decide among these choices, I wrote a dog's inner monolog. At the end of the workshop, she said to me, "You could do this."

I took Paula up on this a decade later, when I accepted her gracious invitation to be a visiting student in her graduate playwriting program at Brown University. *Please Write* was already brewing by then, but the stylistic and emotional risks that the novel eventually took were directly influenced by Paula's lessons in playing "games in order not to look directly into the sun" and "making the familiar strange and the strange familiar."

Further optimistic support came from writer Diane Cole, who led by example, and Bonnie Lederman, for her wise counsel and for being one of the most careful — and caring — readers I know.

Janet Boss, co-founder of Best Friends Dog Obedience, was an important resource. Norman Zagier — arts and entertainment publicist as well as proprietor of Jethro's Dad Dog Care — led me to change this book's title to one that is both more poignant and appropriate.

Karol Menzie, retired *Baltimore Sun* writer and editor, brought me into the Ofteners writing group: Alex Duvan, Lauren Goodsmith, Lucy Hoopes, Sandy Kelman, Judy Tanner, and Clark Riley (computer whiz and novelist with a knack for creating strong female protagonists). The group's over-and-above assistance included Lucy and her granddaughter Emily cooking some of the recipes for my dogs and Karol accompanying me to a variety of dog events.

I owe an additional debt of gratitude to writers Elaine Weiss, James Magruder, Lynn Landay Rosenberg, David Beaudouin, Alison Chaplin, Christine Stewart, and Faith Sullivan. Linda Megathlin, a talented artist, also amped up my imagination, and musician Peggy Pascal provided enthusiastic recommendations.

Thanks also to the highly creative literary family of Tom Hall, Linell Smith, and their gifted playwright daughter, Miranda Rose Hall.

So many friends cheered me on along the way. Forgive any omissions, but among the cheerleaders were Risa Schuster; Karen Beaudouin; Amy and Brian Applestein; Sarah Gillen and Penny Hammar (classmates at Laurel School, an institution that changed my life for the better); Sandy Disner and Nora Manella (classmates at Wellesley College); Andrea Clemente and Stephen Siegforth (skilled editors and treasured neighbors); Ann Saunders (another treasured neighbor); Emma Snyder (owner of Baltimore's premiere independent bookstore, the Ivy Bookshop); and the sibling pep squad of Julie, Katie, and Joey Fink.

Former *Sun* colleagues Stephen Hunter and Kevin Cowherd encouraged me to query Bancroft Press publisher Bruce Bortz, who had previously published books of theirs.

Bruce's powerful belief in *Please Write* extended to every detail, especially the beautiful work of artists Christine Van Bree, Mary Grace Corpus, and Zoe Norvell, and the delightful narration of Nancy Dhulipala, who recorded the audio book.

But perhaps the best evidence of Bruce's belief came in April when he sent me an email whose subject line read: "Your (Damn) Book Made Me Do It: Our First Dog." Yep, undeterred — possibly even inspired — by Zippy's high jinks, Bruce rescued a dog. It is my earnest hope that this book will similarly inspire other readers to welcome a pup into their homes.

Jerry Jackson photographed the subject of one of my proudest *Baltimore Sun* assignments, a profile of Stephen Sondheim. The Broadway legend loved Jerry's photos, and I love the photos he took for this book. (Who else could have coaxed my photo-shy Boston Terrier, Juno, into posing so winsomely?)

Juno is the latest in a long line of Boston Terriers that have graced my life. My detours from the breed have included rescue terriers, one mostly and one partly Jack Russell. Their combined antics are the source of much of the mischief described in this book.

And, with deep love and appreciation to my husband, Alan Fink. Alan had never owned a dog before we met. Since then, he has not only become a dog lover, but he kept after me to complete this novel with the tenacity of a terrier with a bone.

About the Author

J. WYNN ROUSUCK is the theater critic at Baltimore's NPR affiliate, WYPR, and the former longtime theater critic at *The Baltimore Sun*. She has been published in magazines ranging from *American Theatre* to *Dog World*, and her writing has been honored by organizations including the Dog Writers Association of America.

She has taught writing and theater at the Eugene O'Neill Theater Center's National Critics Institute, Goucher College, and in various programs at Johns Hopkins University.

Her award-winning short stories have appeared in *Atticus Review* and *Creative Loafing Tampa Bay*, and her interviews can be found in the books, *Hairspray: The Roots* and *Conversations with Neil Simon*.

A graduate of Wellesley College and the Columbia University Graduate School of Journalism, she was a National Endowment for the Humanities Journalism Fellow at the University of Michigan and a visiting student in the graduate playwriting program at Brown University.

Please Write is part of her family heritage: Her father was a dog judge and his oldest brother wrote one of the first books about Boston Terriers.

She lives in Baltimore with her husband, Alan Fink, and their Boston Terrier, Juno. *Please Write* is her first novel.

www.jwynnrousuck.com